"What's wrong, Kate? Who was on the phone?"

Kate sank onto her sofa and dropped her head into her hands. She looked so upset that Riggs wanted to take her in his arms and hold her.

"He said, 'Back off, Kate, or next time your fireman boyfriend won't be able to save you.'"

Riggs went cold inside. The caller was watching Kate. Now.

Through the window, he scanned the yard and street, searching for movement, a car, a match striking or a cigarette glowing in the dark.

"Do you see anyone?"

The hair on the nape of Riggs's neck stood on end. "No. But he's out there somewhere."

Kate ran her fingers through her hair, sighing wearily.

Riggs's heart stuttered with tenderness for her, and he cupped her face in his hands. "Don't worry, Kate. He's not going to get to you."

THE SECRET
SHE KEPT

—

USA TODAY Bestselling Author
RITA HERRON

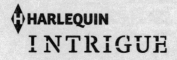

To my fabulous editor, Allison, who has been a steadfast
supporter over the years! Thanks for helping me publish with
Harlequin Intrigue and for always being open to my ideas.

Recycling programs
for this product may
not exist in your area.

ISBN-13: 978-1-335-40164-9

The Secret She Kept

Copyright © 2021 by Rita B. Herron

This edition published by arrangement with Harlequin Books S.A.

For questions and comments about the quality of this book,
please contact us at CustomerService@Harlequin.com.

Harlequin Enterprises ULC
22 Adelaide St. West, 40th Floor
Toronto, Ontario M5H 4E3, Canada
www.Harlequin.com

Printed in U.S.A.

USA TODAY bestselling author **Rita Herron** wrote her first book when she was twelve but didn't think real people grew up to be writers. Now she writes so she doesn't have to get a real job. A former kindergarten teacher and workshop leader, she traded storytelling to kids for writing romance, and now she writes romantic comedies and romantic suspense. Rita lives in Georgia with her family. She loves to hear from readers, so please visit her website, ritaherron.com.

Books by Rita Herron

Harlequin Intrigue

A Badge of Courage Novel

The Secret She Kept

A Badge of Honor Mystery

Mysterious Abduction
Left to Die
Protective Order
Suspicious Circumstances

Badge of Justice

Redemption at Hawk's Landing
Safe at Hawk's Landing
Hideaway at Hawk's Landing
Hostage at Hawk's Landing

Cold Case at Camden Crossing
Cold Case at Carlton's Canyon
Cold Case at Cobra Creek
Cold Case in Cherokee Crossing

Visit the Author Profile page at Harlequin.com.

CAST OF CHARACTERS

Kate McKendrick—Kate blames herself for the school shooting that killed her mother.

Riggs Benford—He will risk his life to save Kate.

Billy Hodgkins—Did he help his brother Ned plan the school shooting?

Woody Mathis—Did he try to kill Kate by sabotaging her car?

Trey Cushing—Did he give Ned the gun he used to shoot his classmates?

Don Gaines—Why doesn't the mayor's son want the past dredged up?

Cassidy Fulton—Does she know if Ned had an accomplice?

Roy Fulton—His mother is keeping secrets.

Prologue

They were all to blame.

Anger churned inside him as he stared at the invitation in his hand.

You are cordially invited to the dedication for the new Briar Ridge High School.

Please join us as we dedicate the building to those who were lost in the Briar Ridge High shooting. Let's celebrate the beginning of a new era!

Kate McKendrick, Principal, Briar Ridge High

He balled his hands into fists. Fifteen years ago, the shooting at the school had torn the town apart. Four students had been killed, along with a teacher. Several others had been injured. Ned Hodgkins, the gunman, had turned the weapon on himself.

His classmates had seemed shocked that Ned would do such a thing. They'd been too busy attending football games, dances, and socializing to notice that Ned had been hurting.

That others had felt left out, too.

He opened the yearbook and cut out photos of all the classmates who'd wronged Ned. Who'd wronged him. One by one, he carefully spread the pictures on his kitchen table.

They were so popular back then. But they'd been selfish.

He tapped the picture of Kate with his finger. She'd wanted to tear down the old school. To destroy the past. To wipe it away as if it never happened.

She had to pay for that.

So did the others. Each would receive their own message. But he'd start with Kate.

He turned the invitation over and began to write.

Dear Kate,
It was your fault.

He placed the invitation back inside the envelope to send to her. She wanted to forget about the past. To pretend Ned wasn't important.

No one would forget about Ned or what had happened.

He wouldn't let them.

Chapter One

Kate McKendrick would never forget the terrible day Ned Hodgins shot up Briar Ridge High School. Sometimes the pain was so unbearable she couldn't breathe.

But she was a survivor. And even though surviving brought guilt, it also inspired her to do something positive for the town where she'd grown up.

Fifteen years had passed now. It was time to move on.

The sound of bus engines roaring to life blended with cheers of students as they left the building. Through her window, she watched the kids high-fiving and gathering by their vehicles to plan where they would go to celebrate.

Summer break was always exciting and meant lazy days at the river, burgers and milkshakes at Frosty's, and swimming at the swimming hole near the falls. Teachers were also anxious for a much-needed vacation from the classroom. Yet this year, the end of the school session marked the beginning of a new era.

Students and faculty would be in a new school come fall. A facility she'd pushed for as the school principal for over two years.

Not only was this old building crumbling around them, but the creek had overflowed and flooded the school. Inspectors had found mold in the walls and the health department had ruled the place a hazard, prompting the building plans to be expedited.

Truthfully, though, the parents in Briar Ridge didn't consider the school a safe place anyway. The shooting that had shattered the town still haunted residents like a black plague.

Mixed emotions filled Kate as the noise outside died down. Inside, the school felt suddenly empty. Cold. Almost eerie.

She left her office, walked into the hall and studied the memorial featuring the students who'd been lost in the shooting. Photographs of the victims hung on the wall. So many lives lost and destroyed that day. So senseless.

But the most personal loss for Kate was her mother, Elaine—a teacher at the time. Forty-five years old. Dead too soon.

She'd taken a bullet to save her students.

Kate blinked back tears. At the time, her mother's dark brown hair hadn't grayed yet, and her smile lit up the room. Every time Kate walked by her mother's English Lit classroom, she could see her mother at the chalkboard, hear her voice as she encouraged students to write their own stories.

Grief clogged her throat as memories taunted her. Her mother dancing around the kitchen at home as she helped Kate and her two best friends, Macy Stark and Brynn Gaines, stir up a batch of chocolate-chip cookies when they were little. Her mother making silly faces as they decorated Christmas stockings, made clothespin reindeer and glittery ornaments. Her mother's off-key singing as she belted out show tunes in the shower.

But the bad memories of the shooting bombarded her, obliterating the sweetness.

Kate could still hear the screams of the terrified kids when Ned Hodgkins unleashed his rage on his classmates with that .38 Special. Athletic Riggs Benford dropping to the floor as a bullet pierced his leg. Mickey Lawson's howl of pain as Ned shot him in the face. Ned turning the gun toward her and Macy. Her mother stepping between them…

Then she was falling, blood gushing from her chest where the bullet pierced her heart….

Reeling with shock, Kate fell to her knees by her mother's side, pressed her hands to her mother's chest and tried to stop the bleeding. Panicked students raced out the door and jumped through windows to escape. Ned barreled down the hallway, shooting wildly.

"Hang in there, Mama," Kate cried.

Tears blurred her mother's eyes, the unconditional love she gave to everyone shining through the pain. She squeezed Kate's hand. "Help the others, honey."

Kate shook her head. She couldn't leave her mother.

But her mother cupped Kate's face in her shaky hands. Hands that had tended to Kate's booboos and comforted her when she was sick or upset. "I love you, Kate. Go. The other kids need you."

What could she do? She was weak, unarmed, couldn't take down a shooter. But the sound of another gunshot bled through the shock immobilizing her. Then more gunfire and screams.

Her mother squeezed her hand again. "Be strong, Kate. Make something good come of this."

Choking back a sob, she ripped off her jacket, folded it and pressed it to her mother's chest. How could anything good come of this horrible, senseless violence?

"Hold on, Mom. Please... I love you."

Just as her mother told her to do, Kate ran to help the injured. Two students were carrying another guy toward the exit. A freshman was huddled in the corner, rocking herself back and forth. Kate helped her up and ushered her into the chem lab to hide. Rushing back to the hall, she searched for her friends Brynn and Macy, but didn't see them. Kids bumped into her as they ran for the doors. Another freshman had fallen in the stampede, and Kate dragged her to the side then helped her up. As the girl ran for the exit, Kate moved on down the hall. Cara Winthrop lay on the floor near the cafeteria, her body still, eyes lifeless. Her boyfriend, Jay Lakewood, held her in his arms, rocking her and crying.

Finally, a siren wailed outside. Police stormed in. An ambulance arrived, medics and firefighters hurrying in to help the wounded.

Kate raced back to check on her mother, but she was too late.

Her mother looked ghostly white, her eyes staring wide open in death.

OUTSIDE THE SCHOOL, the sound of car engines bursting to life and peeling from the parking lot jarred Kate back to the present. Her breathing was erratic and she was shaking. But she looked out and saw clouds forming in the sky, casting a grayness over the treetops.

The last of the staff was also leaving.

Tonight, the mayor had called a town meeting to address recent unrest about the plans for the new school.

When she was a little girl, Briar Ridge had been a sweet, sleepy little vacation mountain town where tourists flocked for the apple and pumpkin festivals in the fall and the Dogwood Festival in the spring. Located a few miles from Bear Mountain, winter vacationers came for skiing and tubing on the mountain.

Bear Mountain still attracted the winter crowd, but people tended to skirt Briar Ridge and each year the festivals had grown smaller and smaller. Plans for new construction and homes had dwindled in the oppressive atmosphere.

In honor of her mother, Kate wanted to help restore Briar Ridge to its former glory.

Suddenly anxious to leave the deserted building, she ducked into her office to finish her paperwork before she left for the day. She noticed a stack of mail that still needed sorting. One particular envelope caught her eye because it had no postage mark. A stamp of the school logo, a black bear, marked the outside.

Nerves clawed at her as she opened the envelope and removed the invitation to the dedication for the new school. Her staff had mailed them to the entire Briar Ridge alumni.

Someone had crumpled the invitation, then refolded it and stuck it back inside the envelope.

Frowning, she flipped it over and stared at the scrawled writing on the back.

Dear Kate,
It was your fault.

Her hand shook as she searched for a signature. But it was blank.

RIGGS BENFORD STOWED his helmet and bunker gear at the firehouse, muttered goodbye to his captain and headed outside to his pickup.

He climbed into the cab, started the engine and drove toward the cabin he'd built four years ago on the edge of town. The scent of smoke and sweat permeated his skin from the fire at the abandoned chicken houses a few miles north of Briar Ridge. He definitely needed a shower before the town meeting.

The guys at the house had been talking about it all day. Locals were still divided over supporting the new build or rallying to repair the existing problems at the old school and turn it into a viable building, perhaps a community center. Although that fight had been lost two years ago, they wanted their voices to be heard. Some even badmouthed Kate McKendrick for pushing the project through.

He hoped things didn't get out of control tonight.

An image of Kate with that fiery red hair taunted him. In high school, she'd been quiet and had kept to herself. Not his type at all. And she sure as hell wouldn't have run around with a guy with the bad reputation he had.

She'd changed since high school, though. Instead of allowing the tragedy that had taken her mother to destroy her, the young, awkward girl had become a leader in the community.

In spite of the fact that he didn't share her optimism, Riggs admired her for instigating positive changes.

The town had been mired in despair for over a decade. Not that anyone should forget the tragedy that had shattered lives, families and friendships, and stolen the innocence of children that day. But living in fear had taken its toll.

Once, people in Briar Ridge had been friendly and welcoming. They'd never locked their doors. Kids had ridden their bikes to the malt shop freely. And when school started each fall, students had raced to class in anticipation of attending football games, pep rallies and school dances.

Now, a wariness pervaded the residents and students.

Hell, he understood that wariness. He'd been a senior at the time and had been shot in the leg. He was one of the lucky ones, though. Sure, he'd had surgery and undergone months of physical therapy to walk again, but he'd recovered physically. Still, his soccer career had come to a halt in spite of the PT and he'd had nightmares of the shooting for months afterward.

Other students hadn't fared so well. The mayor's daughter Brynn had been paralyzed from the waist down. Stone Lawson's younger brother Mickey had been blinded. Another guy had PTSD and had turned

to drugs. Some who'd lost loved ones had moved away
while others couldn't bear to leave the area, as if leaving meant dishonoring the dead.

Even though Kate's mother had died, Kate had stayed
in Briar Ridge. Mrs. McKendrick was the best teacher
he'd ever had. No one knew he'd had trouble reading.
Dyslexia. Kids had teased him when he was young.
Called him stupid. Even his old man had when he was
drunk, which was most days.

But Kate's mother had recognized his problem and
tutored him in private.

She'd also tended his injuries a few times when his
old man had beaten the hell out of him. No one knew
about that, either. He'd begged her to keep it that way.
Still, she'd talked to his mother. Fat lot of good that
had done. When she'd tried to reason with his father,
he'd turned his fists on her. Said she was nothing but
a dumb seamstress. She'd worked at the sewing plant
and made quilts to sell on the side. Riggs had thought
they were pretty.

His father had said she was worthless.

Then one day she'd had enough and she'd cut and
run.

His old man had blamed him for that, too. When
Riggs had been shot, his old man had said he was weak.
He'd left, too.

Didn't matter. He hadn't wanted him around anyway.

Shaking off the memories, Riggs parked at his house,
grabbed his mail and hurried inside. The invitation to
the dedication hung on his fridge, a reminder of the
meeting tonight, and that alumni were coming to town

for a reunion. Guilt for how he'd treated Ned Hodgkins gnawed at him. Ned hadn't fit into the group of jocks he'd hung out with.

They should have been nicer to him, though, but they'd been young and stupid. They'd never considered how adversely their behavior had affected Ned. No one had.

Until it was too late.

They'd been paying for it ever since.

THE WIND WHISTLED shrilly off Bear Mountain, storm clouds casting a gray across the town as Kate veered into the parking lot at the town hall. Some of the older businesses had fallen into disrepair. Awnings and buildings needed painting, as if they, too, felt the weight of the town's burden. Even the town hall needed a facelift.

Trees swayed in the wind, scattering dust and debris; a soda can someone had discarded rolled across the street. Cars and trucks filled the lot, indicating a crowd had showed up for the meeting.

A frisson of nerves slithered through Kate. She hoped the attendees were congenial but braced herself for animosity. The climate over the changes she'd proposed and pushed through had created an avalanche of mixed reactions for months.

Shoulders knotted, she scanned the parking lot in search of trouble. People gathered on the steps to the building, while others hovered beneath the live oaks, hunched in conversation.

The cryptic message she'd received replayed in her

mind. She leaned her forehead against her steering wheel and inhaled a calming breath.

It was your fault.

God... She had blamed herself so many times for her mother's death. For Ned going ballistic.

Two days before the shooting, he'd invited her to the school dance. She'd been so engrossed in studying for her SATs that she'd said no without giving it a second thought.

According to Ned's brother Billy, her rejection had tipped him over the edge.

A car honked and she jerked her head up. A red Trans Am veered into the parking lot, tires squealing. Billy Hodgkins threw open the door, unfolded his beefy body from the front of the car, and strode toward the door, pulling at his wooly beard. The scowl on his face sent chills down her spine. Billy and his family had moved away a few months after the shooting to escape the negative publicity and hate in the town.

But she'd never forgotten his accusations.

A gust of wind whipped at her car, and thunder rumbled in the distance. She checked her watch. Time to go inside and face the crowd.

Her mother's last words echoed in her head. *Be strong, Kate. Make something good come of this.*

She couldn't make anything good come of it. But she could try to help people move past the pain and concentrate on the future.

Another gust of wind swirled around her as she slid from her car, and she shoved her hair from her face. Determined to remain positive, she strode up the steps to the town hall and went inside. Voices and chatter rumbled from the main meeting room, and a family passed her as they entered. She took another breath, pasted on a smile and ducked into the room.

The town council members and Amy Turner, the former school counselor and head of the memorial committee, were seated on stage at the front of the room, where a seat awaited her. Amy had been in her midthirties when the shooting occurred. Like many others, she felt responsible for not recognizing the depth of Ned's depression.

She'd also reached out to Kate after her mother's death and had helped her through the grieving process.

Mayor Gaines was addressing the council as she hurried down the side aisle. Chatter and voices reverberated around her. An argument heated up somewhere near the back, and she saw Billy trying to push his way past two other men blocking his entry.

Sheriff Stone Lawson was perched in the rear by one of the doors. His deputy, Murphy Bridges, stood on the opposite side, braced to handle problems if tempers escalated out of control. Stone and Murphy had been classmates and now worked to maintain order in the town.

As Billy entered, he aimed a menacing look toward Kate.

Fear fluttered in her belly as she took her seat.

Be strong, Kate.

I'm trying, Mama.

Mayor Gaines called the meeting to order then introduced the council members. "Tonight, we're here to discuss the plans for our new school. As you all know, due to the dilapidated state of the high school and the costly repairs necessary to ensure the safety of our children's health, the town council approved the funding for a new facility a while back and the new building is almost finished."

Disgruntled whispers floated through the room. Kate surveyed the group. The parents of the victims who'd died that day were present, along with family members of the ones injured. Brynn sat in the front row by her mother, her face pale, hands clenched around the arms of her wheelchair.

Kate's heart gave a pang. She missed their friendship. But when she'd dropped by the hospital to see Brynn after the shooting, Mrs. Gaines had warned Kate to stay away from Brynn. She'd tried to visit multiple times those first few months and over the years, but Mrs. Gaines had repeatedly claimed Brynn didn't want to see her.

The woman's animosity only intensified Kate's guilt. How could Brynn forgive her for causing Ned to shoot up the school and put her in that wheelchair?

Taking deep breaths to control her emotions, she continued to scan the room.

Riggs Benford was seated behind Brynn. His big body exuded sexuality and was a palpable force of strength and energy in the room.

Kate dragged her gaze away from him. She'd always had a crush on him, but Riggs was brooding one minute and a player the next. She'd put him in the off-limits category long ago. A place where he would always stay. The fact that he'd abandoned his teenage girlfriend when she was pregnant disturbed her. But he was a kid at the time and his behavior could be forgiven.

The fact that he'd never taken responsibility for his son couldn't.

Her own father had done the same thing to her. Even though she'd never known him, it hurt to think he hadn't wanted her.

Still, Riggs wasn't all bad. He'd overcome his own injury, one that had ended his hopes of a soccer scholarship, and now he ran into burning buildings to save others.

The mayor gestured to a man seated in the front row, drawing her attention back to the meeting.

"Local builder and developer Carlton Ethridge has worked with us as an architect on the designs. Many of you already know Realtor Ling Wu, who grew up right here in Briar Ridge. Ling helped us secure a nice piece of property that offers room for growth in the future."

Someone made a rude noise. Mayor Gaines tensed. "I'm aware some of you have reservations about tearing down the old school, but please hear Principal McKendrick out. She cares about our community and our children." He tipped his head toward Kate.

She maneuvered her way to the podium, gripped the edge to steady herself, then forced a smile.

"First of all, I appreciate the fact that so many of you came tonight. I understand the town has been divided emotionally over this issue, but I believe a new building will facilitate goodwill and positive changes for all the residents and future visitors."

"You just want to forget what happened," someone shouted.

"That's not true," Kate said. "I was a student at Briar Ridge High myself. My own mother, a teacher at the school, died during the massacre. I can never forget what happened that day, nor do I believe that any of us should." Her voice rose, filled with conviction. "Lives were not only lost, but families and friendships ripped apart. Students suffered emotional trauma as well as physical injuries. None of us will ever be the same."

"That school is a monument to the ones who didn't survive," a woman cried. "My son was one of them."

Kate's heart ached for the woman, Linda Russell. Her sixteen-year-old son Hughie had had dreams of med school. Yet the building was falling apart just as the town was. "I understand that, and we're creating another memorial for the victims and their families at the new building, one I think you'll all be proud of. We plan to reveal the details at the dedication ceremony."

She glanced across the group, that cryptic message haunting her. Had someone in this room sent it?

Chapter Two

"You expect us to forget that our children died," Harold Guthrie bellowed.

In spite of his accusation, sympathy for the man welled inside Kate. Harold's seventeen-year-old daughter Agnes had been Ned's third victim. A bullet had pierced her aorta.

Kate shook her head. "No one here will ever forget that tragedy, Mr. Guthrie. But I believe it's beneficial for today's students to stop living in fear, fear created because our town still dwells on that devastating event." She pressed her hand over her chest. "That tragedy defined us, but we can't let it destroy us."

"Tearing down the school won't wipe out our grief or bring back our children," a man in the back row yelled.

"It won't stop us from being afraid when we send our babies to school," another woman shouted.

"I can't promise we won't have trouble again. No one can," Kate said earnestly. "But rest assured, we're incorporating security measures to make Briar Ridge High as safe as possible."

A tall man Kate didn't recognize stood and aimed a

look at Jose Fernandez, one of the refugees who'd attended the school the year of the shooting. "Terrorists get guns past security all the time."

"My son is not a terrorist," Jose's mother said angrily.

Suddenly protests erupted.

Riggs Benford stood and waved his hand. "Kate is right. Being held hostage to fear is not living at all. We can honor those who've fallen with the new building."

The mayor's wife shot up from her seat. "It's easy for you to say that because you survived and can still walk. My daughter is confined to that chair."

"Mother!" Brynn grabbed at her mother's arm in an attempt to force her to sit. Her look of horror made Kate want to comfort her as they'd comforted each other as kids. But she sensed Brynn wouldn't want that now.

The outburst escalated, angry accusations flying through the room over who was to blame for Ned's breakdown.

The cryptic note Kate received earlier was burned into her brain. She attempted to regain control of the meeting, but no one was listening. A heated exchange in the back erupted and one man raised a fist.

Sheriff Lawson rushed to stop a fight from breaking out while Deputy Bridges made an effort to calm others. Kate's pulse pounded and she slowly backed away from the podium. Images of her classmates running and screaming flashed behind her eyes.

Her mother's blood…

The rage, and then the blank look in Ned's eyes, as if he hadn't quite comprehended what he'd done.

The gun turning on her…

Suddenly she couldn't breathe. She'd suffered from panic attacks for months after the shooting. She was on the verge of one now.

Her gaze met Riggs's for a second. Concern darkened his eyes and he stepped forward. Humiliation washed over her. She couldn't have a meltdown in front of him or any of these people.

The room was blurring, lights flickering wildly, colors fading to black. She pushed past the other town council members and clawed her way to the side door. Instead of heading toward the front entrance where she'd have to deal with the angry crowd, she staggered toward the rear exit.

RIGGS HAD SEEN enough hotheads in his lifetime, and he didn't like the atmosphere in the room. Hell, he'd been worried about protestors, but the situation was quickly escalating to the point of violence.

Sheriff Lawson and his deputy worked to calm the outburst, and Riggs decided to check on Kate. She hadn't deserved to be under attack, not after all she'd suffered and lost.

And certainly not because of her good intentions. He'd heard she'd instigated measures to stop bullying in school and to keep troubled kids from falling through the cracks. Just like her mother, she cared about students.

And God knew, he owed her mother.

As he wove his way to the front door, he spotted classmates he hadn't seen in over a decade. Jay Lakewood, then Duke Eastman. He'd been buddies with them back in the day, but they'd lost touch over the years. He'd heard Jay had joined the military and become a bomb expert. Duke was a Navy SEAL.

Gretta Wright, another former classmate, who currently worked for the local news station, darted toward a group of angry protestors with her microphone. Gretta had started a gossip rag in high school and had made more enemies than friends whenever she threw anyone in her path under the bus for a byline.

He cut a wide berth around her and stepped into the lobby. Jay and Duke strode toward him.

"Hey, man, long time no see," Jay said.

Duke pounded him on the back. "I saw the way you were looking at Kate. Do you have something going on with her?" he asked with a chuckle.

Riggs snorted. "She barely gives me the time of day when I see her around town."

"Guess it's your reputation as a ladies' man," Jay said with a grin.

Riggs's gut tightened. His old friend was probably right. He had made mistakes, mistakes that had cost him. "That was a long time ago. I'm not the same guy I was in high school."

Duke rubbed a hand over his stomach where his scar from the shooting would have been. "None of us is."

A tense silence fell between them for a minute, the memories returning. Good and bad.

"I'm surprised to see you two here," Riggs said.

Jay shrugged. "Figured it was time I got up the courage to come back."

That admission surprised Riggs. "You work with bombs. I didn't think you were afraid of anything."

Jay flexed his hands and looked at them, his expression strained. Riggs felt like a heel for his callous remark. Jay had escaped physically unhurt from the school shooting but psychological scars ran deep.

While Riggs had lain writhing in pain, Jay had run to tackle Ned to get his gun. But Ned had grabbed Jay's girlfriend, Cara Winthrop, as a hostage and forced everyone to back off. Then he'd shot Cara five times.

Jay had beaten himself up for years, saying he should have saved Cara.

But no one could have saved her.

"How about we grab a beer and catch up?" Duke suggested.

Riggs hesitated. "Rain check? I need to get going."

They exchanged cell numbers before Riggs hurried through the exit. The scent of impending rain swirled around him as he paused on the steps and scanned the parking lot for Kate's black SUV. He spotted it, but Kate wasn't inside.

Worry knotted his belly. She'd had time to make it to her vehicle by now. Where was she?

Adrenaline pumping through him, he darted down the steps then around the side of the structure. The parking lot was full, several people heading to their cars, some deep in conversation, others ranting about Kate.

The urge to shut them up slammed into him, but he resisted. Violence wasn't the answer.

After he'd recovered from the shooting and worked

through his self-pity, he'd made it his life's work to save people, not hurt them.

Worry tightened his muscles as he jogged toward the rear of the building. Kate stood on the back stoop, leaning against the railing. She looked pale, her hands clenching the iron bars as if she needed them to hold her up.

Billy Hodgkins crept up behind Kate, his beady eyes practically disappearing in his face beneath that bushy beard. He looked like a mountain man, wild and dangerous, a predator about to pounce on his prey.

Protective instincts surged through Riggs. "Kate?" Riggs rushed toward the stoop.

Billy's head jerked up and he darted back inside the building.

Riggs climbed the bottom step. "Are you okay?"

She seemed dazed, even confused, but slowly shook her head and looked down at him. Something deep and unsettling stirred in Riggs's chest.

He'd seen that frightened look in his mama's eyes just before his daddy unleashed his temper on her. He'd hated it then.

He hated it now.

Not that Kate was fragile. But at the moment, she looked so vulnerable and frightened, he had the insane urge to pull her into his arms and hold her.

A ridiculous thought. Kate didn't even like him.

Riggs offered his hand to her. "Let me walk you to your car."

She moved down a step, but didn't accept his hand,

proving he was right. Even when she was scared, Kate didn't want anything to do with him.

KATE DRAGGED IN AIR, still battling the panic. The moment she heard Billy mutter her name, déjà vu struck her with the force of a blow to her chest.

"What did Billy say to you?" Riggs asked.

Kate bit her lower lip.

"Did he threaten you?" Riggs pressed.

Had Billy threatened her? She hadn't heard exactly what he'd said. Then Riggs had appeared. "I...he mumbled something, but I didn't catch his exact words."

"I don't trust him," Riggs said.

"Neither do I. He has a right to be at the meeting, though," she said in a low voice. "He suffered, too. His family had to live in the shadow of what Ned did."

Riggs muttered an obscenity. "Don't be naïve, Kate. That guy's a bully and always has been."

She shrugged but tensed at his tone. "Maybe. But he lost his brother that day. And everyone in town and at school treated him like he was a killer, too."

Except he'd blamed her. And, unknowingly at the time, she'd played a role in Ned's breakdown.

They reached her SUV and she leaned against the driver's door and looked up at him. Riggs had been popular in high school. As soon as he'd broken up with one girl, a string of others lined up to take her place. As far as she knew, he was still a womanizer. With his good looks and charm, women fell at his feet.

She didn't intend to be one of them.

Still, he'd turned into a town hero. And it was impossible not to notice the smoky hue of his dark brown eyes.

"I figured some people would be emotional about the demolition of the old building," Kate said. "But I didn't expect the bitterness that's surfaced."

"The town has been steeped in grief and anger for years, Kate. It's time someone forced everyone to move on."

Kate sighed. "I just want Briar Ridge to be a happy place again, for it to be like it was when I was little."

Riggs clenched his jaw. "After all that's happened, I can't believe you look at life through rose-colored glasses."

Kate tensed. He had no idea how she struggled with finding the positive. "Better than seeing the bad in everyone."

She reached inside her purse for her keys before she did something stupid like lean into Riggs for support. Her keys jangled as she removed them from her bag.

Riggs's dark gaze searched her face. "Why don't I follow you home?"

The earlier message, then the animosity at the meeting, and seeing Billy again, had shaken her to the core.

Sexy bad boy Riggs Benford was a danger of another kind.

She couldn't interpret his concern for anything more.

"I'm fine, Riggs. Thanks for walking me to my car." She didn't wait for a response. She slid into the driver's seat and waved goodbye, then slowly backed from the parking spot. More than one vehicle gave a rude honk as she passed.

Only a few days until the dedication for the new building. She refused to allow a few disgruntled residents to keep her from implementing her plans.

With the news constantly reporting about mass shootings in other cities and towns, nerves ran high. Several students this year had visited the counselor because of anxiety issues over attending school. Students deserved to feel safe and happy. Parents deserved it, too.

A momentary tug of longing enveloped her. She didn't have children herself but her biological clock was ticking, and sometimes she imagined having a little one of her own. A baby nestled in her arms. A home…

But with the craziness in the world and seeing it firsthand, she was afraid to love and lose again.

Maneuvering her way onto Main Street, she passed the park situated in the heart of town, then the library, hardware store, the ice cream shop, the Mercantile, Pearl's Dine & Pie, Joy's Fabric and Crafts, and the empty lot where the church sold pumpkins in the fall and Christmas trees in November and December.

Headlights behind her nearly blinded her, and she slowed and checked the rearview mirror. She couldn't make out the car or tell if it was following her. But it was too close for comfort.

Irritated, she pulled over in front of Briar Ridge Inn. For a moment, the car slowed beside her, and she felt eyes piercing her. She didn't recognize the dark sedan, but it was a common make and model. With dozens of visitors in town, it could even be a rental.

Finally, the car moved on. She breathed a sigh of relief then veered back onto the road. She'd almost reached her street when she smelled smoke. A second later, the scent of gas assaulted her.

Pulse clamoring, she checked the rearview mirror. Smoke seeped from the rear near the gas tank. Panic seized her. She jerked the SUV to the side of the road, threw it in Park and jumped out.

Just as her feet hit the graveled shoulder, her car burst into flames.

Chapter Three

Riggs had no idea why he was so anxious about Kate.
But he despised seeing any woman attacked, physically
or verbally. And some of the locals had practically assaulted her at the meeting.

Billy Hodgkins especially worried him.

Kate might believe the Hodgkins family had gotten an unfair shake, but Billy had always been trouble.
Unlike his weaker brother Ned, Billy used his muscles
and foul mouth to intimidate.

He'd heard Billy was a mean drunk, too. What if he
showed up at Kate's?

*She's not your responsibility. She doesn't even like
you.*

Still, he didn't turn around. He'd just stop by to see
that she'd made it home safely.

An image of Kate in front of that podium taunted
him, her glossy auburn hair shimmering over her shoulders, her delicate little chin jutted up as she pleaded
her cause.

In high school, she'd been quiet, shy, bookish. Some
kids had called her Kate the Brainiac. Other horny idi-

ots had made crude comments about her big boobs and curves, which had made her blush. They'd wanted in her pants.

Like any red-blooded teenage boy, he'd fantasized about having sex with her, too. But Kate wasn't the type to sleep around. Somewhere deep inside, the crude comments had irked him. They'd felt...wrong.

Kate was a nice girl, the kind who deserved better than being groped in the back seat of a car.

She'd also avoided him like he was on fire. Obviously, she'd heard the rumors about him knocking up Cassidy Fulton. He had dated Cassidy. A couple of times.

Then he'd learned she was just using him. But he'd never told anyone that part. He'd been too embarrassed, had too much pride, so he'd let everyone think they were an item.

When she'd turned up pregnant a couple of months before the shooting, everyone assumed the kid was his. Hell, he'd thought it was, too. Three months after he was injured, when he was mired deep in self-pity and depression and needed something to live for, he'd insisted on a paternity test. Said if the baby was his, he'd take responsibility and marry Cassidy. But she'd laughed in his face. Told him she'd never marry a cripple.

Then the paternity test proved he wasn't the father. She'd never shared the baby daddy's name, though.

Struggling with physical therapy and the sting of her cruel comment, he hadn't bothered to correct the rumor. Worse, Gretta Wright had spread the news that he'd abandoned Cassidy and her child.

At the time, he'd shrugged it off. Had been ticked off at life and hadn't given a damn what anyone thought about him.

But he was older now and not as shallow. The shooting had changed him. Had literally altered the course of his life.

Not just because he'd taken a bullet. In the chaos of the bloody massacre, he'd felt helpless.

As he'd watched first responders rush to save lives, he'd been awed by their courage. Later, while he lay in bed after surgery, feeling angry and hopeless, one of the firefighters had visited him at the hospital.

That day, Riggs decided he wanted to be like him. Firefighting required skill, physical fitness, as well as mental strength. So, he'd worked his butt off in PT to get back into shape.

Thunder rumbled, storm clouds moving in. He maneuvered a curve then turned onto the street leading to Kate's house. Smoke caught his eye. Thick plumes floated upward into the darkness. Then flames.

Pulse hammering, he pressed the accelerator and sped up. He raced around another curve, made the turn and spotted the source of the fire.

Kate's black SUV.

Fear shot through him as he swerved to the side of the road to park and dialed 9-1-1.

Was Kate inside that vehicle?

COLD FEAR ATE at Kate as she stared at the flames shooting into the sky. Red, yellow, orange…

Fire crackled and popped. Glass shattered. Heat

seared her. Smoke billowed so thick she could barely breathe.

If she'd waited a few seconds longer to get out, she would have been trapped in her car.

Trembling, she reached inside her purse for her phone to call for help.

"Kate!"

A man's voice jarred her, and she spotted Riggs jogging toward her.

Firelight from the flames lit his rugged face as he approached. "Are you all right?"

She nodded numbly.

He gently took her face in his hands as if examining her. "Are you hurt?"

Smoke caught in her throat and she coughed. "No," she said in a ragged whisper.

"What happened?"

"I was driving home and suddenly smelled smoke, so I pulled over." Her legs felt weak, but she stiffened her spine in an attempt to hold herself upright.

Riggs gently rubbed her arms. "Let's move away from the fire." He coaxed her beneath a nearby tree. "Help is on the way."

She leaned against a boulder on the embankment and he knelt beside her, calming her with soft reassurances. Seconds later, a siren wailed, lights twirling against the inky sky.

"Have you had car trouble lately?" Riggs asked.

"No, that's what makes this so odd. I don't understand why it just burst into flames."

Considering the temperament of the meeting and

the animosity toward Kate, suspicions snaked through Riggs.

The wail of sirens grew closer. The firetruck from his own firehouse careened up, the sheriff's squad car on its tail.

The fire engine screeched to a stop and his team jumped from the truck, geared up and ready to work. His buddy Brian spotted him and threw up a hand.

Riggs squeezed Kate's shoulder. "Are you sure you're all right?"

"Yes," Kate said, although the warble to her voice indicated she was anything but okay.

"Stay here. I'll be right back." Riggs rushed over to his friend, who was already pulling a hose from the truck.

"What happened?" Brian asked. "Where's the driver?"

Riggs relayed his conversation with Kate and described the climate at the meeting. "This fire might not be accidental, so look for anything suspicious."

Brian's brow lifted. "You think someone tried to kill Kate?"

Riggs shrugged. "I hope not, but we can't rule it out yet."

Concern flared in his buddy's eyes, and he gave a quick nod. "On it." Brian hurried to join his team.

The sheriff parked and climbed out, his rugged face a scowl as he assessed the situation. Although Riggs had played soccer and Stone football, they'd been friends in school. When Stone's father had passed, Stone had been a no-brainer for sheriff.

A woman emerged from the front seat of Stone's car, her body rigid, face in the shadows.

Riggs's pulse jumped with recognition. Macy Stark. She, Kate and Brynn Gaines were as different as night and day. But as teenagers, they'd been inseparable. He'd been surprised Macy had left town shortly after the shooting.

Had the women stayed in touch?

Stone strode toward Riggs, expression intense. "Where's Kate?"

Riggs pointed to the tree, his gut clenching. She sat hunched against that rock, her arms wrapped around her legs as if she was trying to hold herself together. He expected Macy to race over to Kate, but she remained rooted by Stone's car, eyes assessing, serious, calm but questioning.

"Does she need a doctor?" Stone asked.

"I don't think so. She's just shaken." Heat from the blaze made sweat break out on Riggs's neck.

Or maybe it was fear that Kate's car fire wasn't an accident.

KATE SILENTLY REMINDED herself she was safe. She'd lost her car, but she had insurance. Her SUV could be replaced.

At least no one had been hurt.

For months after the shooting, she'd struggled with survivor's guilt. But losing her mother and seeing classmates die had also taught her to prioritize. A human life, *any* human life, was more valuable than material possessions.

Her breath quickened. Macy was standing by the sheriff's car.

A pang of longing swelled inside Kate. At age seven, she, Macy and Brynn had spit on their hands, rubbed them together and declared themselves spit sisters. For years they'd cried, laughed, and shared secrets together. She'd thought they'd always be friends.

But that was before the shooting.

Kate's shoulders tensed as her gaze met Macy's. Her former best friend had kept her distance at the town meeting. She hadn't voiced an opinion one way or the other about the old school being demolished.

What was she doing here now?

Macy pivoted to look at the fire, and Kate noticed her left arm was in a sling. Macy had been athletic and talked about running track in college and then becoming a coach.

Instead, she'd joined the FBI. Had she been injured on the job?

With a quick glance at Kate, Macy joined the sheriff and Riggs.

Kate fought anger. How could the girl she'd once loved like a sister return to town and ignore her? Macy had deserted her when Kate had needed her most.

Memories of tea parties, sleepovers and playing dress-up in Brynn's mother's ball gowns flooded Kate. The girls had shopped for dresses for their school dances together, never missed a birthday celebration, and had dreamed about their weddings.

She'd heard Macy had married Trey Cushing after college. Kate hadn't been invited to the wedding. And

Trey seemed an odd fit for Macy, but Kate had never gotten the chance to ask her how they'd wound up together.

A wave of sadness washed over Kate. She and Macy had first bonded when they were five. Kate had heard a noise in the yard by her window and thought it was a sick cat. She and her mother ran outside and found Macy hovering by the bushes, scared and sobbing. Macy's mother had locked her out of the house. Another time, Kate recalled, Macy's mother had left her at the park alone.

Both times, Kate's mother had comforted Macy and welcomed her into their house. Once, when she'd driven Macy home, they'd found Macy's mother having an "episode," at least, that was what Macy called it. Later, they'd learned Mrs. Stark was bipolar and had gone off her meds. From then on, Kate and her mother had become Macy's safe haven.

Yet at Kate's mother's funeral, Macy had stood on the edge of the service and stared blankly, as if she hadn't grown up in Kate's house. Brynn had still been in the hospital and had needed Macy, too.

But Macy had abandoned them both.

Kate felt even more alone now because of it.

Finally, Macy looked back at her and, for a moment, her eyes filled with some emotion Kate couldn't define. Regret? Longing?

Blame?

It was your fault.

Whoever sent that message knew Kate's rejection had sent him over the edge.

Ned's brother had known. And he'd told Macy and Brynn.

Did her best friends blame her for the shooting? Was that the reason Macy had left town? And the reason she'd finally come back?

When she looked at Kate, did she see their classmates falling to their deaths?

RIGGS KEPT HIS suspicions about the car fire to himself as he drove Kate home. No need to alarm her until it was confirmed the fire was intentional.

She'd been through enough tonight. The sheer fact that she was riding in the truck with him proved how shaken up she was.

He parked in front of her Craftsman bungalow and cut the engine. Her street was in a quiet little neighborhood where mamas and daddies strolled their babies down the sidewalk and joggers ran with their dogs.

An image of Kate smiling as she sipped sweet iced tea on the front porch gave him a pang in his chest. He wished to hell she'd grace him with that smile. At least once.

Instead she was polite. But she kept her distance.

Not that he blamed her.

A picture of Kate pushing a baby stroller struck him out of the blue. Dammit, he'd never thought about having a family himself. But lately a seed of longing had sprouted inside him. He'd grown…what? Tired of being a bachelor? Bored with waking up alone?

Hell, he wasn't alone. He had friends. Plenty of

women to sleep with, if he was interested. Only lately his interest in one-night stands had dwindled.

The guys at the firehouse were his family. Maybe he'd get a dog.

Kate's soft voice jerked him from his thoughts. "Thanks for the ride, Riggs."

"No problem." He itched to say more, to ask her to invite him in and let him stay with her for a while. Why, he didn't know.

Maybe because she's the one damn woman who's never given you the time of day.

Was he really that big of a jerk?

She reached for the door handle and opened it, and he hurried around to help her out. Dammit, she might not like him, but his job made him wary. What if Billy showed up?

After the shooting, everyone had wondered if Ned'd had an accomplice. Billy had been their prime suspect. What if the publicity about the new school was making Billy nervous and he feared the truth would finally be revealed?

Riggs took Kate's arm as she climbed from his truck, but she tensed and pulled away. "I'm fine, Riggs." He walked silently beside her to the front door.

Her keys jangled as she removed them from her purse, and her hand trembled so badly she dropped them. He hoped to hell the fire had caused her nerves, that she wasn't afraid of *him*.

He might have been a player, but he'd never been rough with a woman. That was his father's MO.

Riggs stooped, snagged the keys and unlocked the

door. "Like it or not, I'm going to look around the house."

Fear clouded her face, making him feel like a heel for putting it there. She dropped her purse on the foyer table then crossed the room to the cushy blue sofa in front of the stacked stone fireplace. "I realize some people are angry with me, but surely no one would break into my house."

She was trusting to a fault. Billy was a loose cannon. Riggs refrained from commenting, though, as he walked through her living room and kitchen. The blue and white décor and farmhouse furniture was tasteful and homey, and the scent of lavender filled the room. His own cabin was more rustic and, although the river ran behind the property, he had very little furniture and no photographs or personal touches. It was just a place to sleep.

Kate sank onto the dark blue sofa, picked up an afghan and began to stroke the blanket. Floor-to-ceiling windows flanked both sides of the fireplace, offering a wooded view of her backyard. She must have chosen the house because it was close enough to the school for a short commute, but the house had been built to accommodate a spectacular view of Bear Mountain.

"It'll just take a minute for me to check the windows and doors," he said.

Wariness crossed her face, but she nodded.

He paused in the hallway to study the photos of Kate and her mother. Mrs. McKendrick had been the only reason he'd passed English Lit. Those private tutoring sessions had helped him save face and keep his position on the soccer team.

Ned had shot him only a few feet away from Kate's mother, who'd stepped in front of Ned to save her students. He'd never forget seeing Kate on her hands and knees sobbing over her mother as she'd tried to stop the bleeding. The screams, the bodies falling…the horror. Even through it, Kate had rushed to help others.

She was still trying to do that.

Shaking off the grisly image of the shooting, Riggs checked the guest bedroom window then the master. The room definitely belonged to a woman. A plush lavender comforter covered a large, white ironwork bed, a watercolor of lilacs on the wall above. Candles sat on the nightstand, the lavender scent stronger in here. The bed drew his eyes, eliciting an image of Kate beneath the decadent covers.

What the hell was wrong with him? This lust for Kate was coming out of nowhere.

Angry with himself, he hurriedly checked the windows then the bathrooms and laundry room, searching for a bomb or trigger mechanism that would send her house up in flames like her car.

You're being paranoid, dude.

Although considering the night's events, maybe he wasn't paranoid at all. If that fire was intentional, someone had just tried to kill Kate.

Chapter Four

A storm was brewing outside, the wind howling off Bear Mountain like a lion roaring. Grateful to be inside, Kate filled the kettle with water to heat for tea.

Having Riggs in her house resurrected teenage insecurities she thought she'd finally overcome. Every girl in school had crushed on him. With his thick dark hair, smoky eyes and that dimple in his right cheek, he was a charmer.

And that body. He'd been fit when he'd played soccer, but the man had gained muscle and grown three more inches. He must be at least six-three because he towered over her and made her feel small, which, at five-seven and with her curves, she wasn't.

She'd never been one of the skinny girls who nibbled on rabbit food and wore crop tops to show off her flat belly like Brynn had done. Brynn's beauty-pageant-coordinator mother had pressured Brynn into near starvation to fit into a size two, so Brynn had always snuck in cookies and pizza at Kate's house before she went home.

Kate had never been a size two and never would be.

Her mother said she'd bloomed early. She'd developed boobs by age eleven, which had drawn ogles from the hormonal boys who interpreted that to mean she was easy. Her hips had followed, giving her curves and an added ten, fifteen pounds. The unwanted attention had heightened her insecurities about her body.

But after high school, she'd worked hard to overcome a negative self-image and hoped to be a role model to other young girls.

Footsteps jerked Kate back to reality, and she squared her shoulders. With his sexy physique and those smoldering eyes, Riggs could have a woman disrobing for him in seconds. But she silently reminded herself that he was not there for personal reasons. He'd simply given her a ride home. For all she knew, his latest love interest might be waiting on him at home tonight. Waiting in his bed...

"Everything looks clear," Riggs said, although he didn't quite meet her eyes when he looked at her. "Do you have a security system?"

"No. I've thought about it, but I always felt safe here." An odd thing to say considering the town had nearly been destroyed by a mass murder. And if Ned had had an accomplice as Stone Lawson's father had suspected, another killer might be hiding in plain sight in Briar Ridge. He could have been there all along.

The teakettle whistled and she quickly turned off the stove. Her hand trembled as she poured hot water into a mug and dunked a tea bag inside.

"Would you like some tea?" she asked. Lame. Riggs was not the tea-sipping kind of man. She turned to face him, eyebrows raised. "Or something stronger? I have whiskey."

A small grin tugged at the corner of his mouth. "I didn't figure you for a whiskey kind of girl."

Kate blushed. "What kind of girl did you figure me for?"

"Tea," he said with a chuckle.

She couldn't resist a comeback. "I might surprise you." Perspiration beaded on her forehead. Had she just flirted with Riggs? Heaven help her. She must be more shaken than she'd thought.

"I have a feeling you're full of surprises, Kate," he murmured in a voice laced with innuendo.

He flirts with every female he meets. Don't let it go to your head.

Determined not to make a fool out of herself, Kate reached inside her cabinet, removed a bottle of Jack Daniel's, added a shot to her tea and poured a finger into a highball glass for him.

Their hands brushed when she gave him the drink, and a thread of desire rippled through her.

Riggs's gaze locked with hers, tension simmering between them. Had he read her reaction?

Of course, he had. He was experienced with women. Smooth.

She was as smooth as cracked glass.

Thankfully, her brain interceded and overrode her silly fantasies. She might have escaped a burning car tonight, but she'd be playing with fire if she imagined Riggs was interested in her. Well…he might be interested in sex just because he liked women—all women—

but it would be nothing more. And she didn't intend to be a notch on his bedpost.

Needing to wrangle her wayward thoughts, she carried her mug to the sofa and sank onto it. Riggs joined her, facing her from the oversize club chair by the fireplace. Somehow, his big body looked comfortable there, like he belonged.

You must have inhaled too much smoke. It's making you light-headed.

"For the record, Kate," Riggs said, his voice gruff, "I think your plans for the school are admirable."

His praise warmed the chill invading her. "Thanks. After my mother died, I stayed in our house for a long time. But everywhere I looked, I saw her ghost. And her perfume was permanently embedded in the walls."

His look darkened. "I know losing her was difficult. She was an amazing woman, and the best teacher I ever had."

"She was a great mother, too, loving and kind and always so positive. I never want to forget her and her sacrifice," Kate said. "But living in that house without her was just so h…ard. I knew Mom wouldn't want me having a pity party." She ran her finger around the rim of her mug and bit her tongue. For heaven's sake, why was she babbling?

Unable to stop herself, though, she continued. "After I finished my Masters, I talked to Amy. She suggested I sell the house and make a fresh start." Kate blew into her tea, lost in thought for a moment as she remembered her initial reaction to the suggestion. "I balked at the idea at first. It felt like I was betraying my mother. That if I moved from our home, I'd forget her." The same way locals were reacting to tearing down the school.

"What changed your mind?"

"Eventually, I realized she would have wanted me to move on and be happy. So I slowly started cleaning out, and discovered it was cathartic. I kept things that were sentimental and looked around for a place to move. The developer was just building the bungalows on this street. Suddenly the prospect of having my own place where I could put my stamp on it excited me." She gestured around the living area and kitchen. "I brought the good memories with me here and decided to build a future that Mom would be proud of."

"That's the reason you pushed so hard for the new school building," Riggs said quietly.

"It's been years. I thought it was time to move on," Kate said "New places inspire new beginnings that can lead to a more positive future."

"People just need time." He sipped his whiskey, drawing her gaze to the long column of his throat as he swallowed.

How could a man's throat possibly be sexy?

Oblivious to her ridiculous thoughts, he leaned forward, his gaze pinning her. She barely resisted the urge to squirm. She had no idea why she'd poured out her personal feelings. Except, Riggs was easy to talk to. And tonight had rattled her and resurrected memories from high school.

Another memory sobered her. Riggs and Cassidy Fulton. Cassidy's son's face flashed in her mind. Roy was a gangly kid who didn't make friends easily. And he desperately needed a father.

But Riggs had never owned up to the fact that he was Roy's father, nor had he been a presence in Roy's life. Just like her own father hadn't.

RIGGS BATTLED THE urge to kiss Kate. Her story had touched his heart.

In spite of his bad boy reputation, he did not take advantage of vulnerable, frightened women.

And judging from the way Kate was avoiding eye contact with him, she wouldn't welcome his lips on hers.

That fact stung, but he wrangled in his libido. If he wanted her to think he was a better man than his father or the lowlife everyone thought him to be for abandoning his teenage pregnant girlfriend, he had to prove it.

Act like a gentleman. Keep his hands to himself.

Even if it killed him.

Talk business. "Kate, other than Billy, is there anyone in particular who'd want to hurt you?"

She ran a hand through the long strands of that wavy auburn hair, making his hands itch to touch it.

"Probably half the folks at that meeting tonight. You heard them." She dropped her hand back to her lap. "The truth is I understand their feelings," she said, compassion flickering in her eyes. "Change is difficult. So is forgiveness."

True. "Have you received any threats lately?"

She worried her bottom lip with her teeth. "Not exactly," she said slowly.

He narrowed his eyes. "What do you mean *not exactly?*"

Indecision played across Kate's face before she set her mug on the coffee table and retrieved her purse. She removed an envelope from inside and offered it to him.

He removed the invitation to the dedication ceremony, confused at first. Then he spotted the hand-scrawled message on the back.

It was your fault.

Anger tightened every muscle in Riggs's body. "When did you get this?"

"Today. It was in the mail at school."

The timing was definitely suspicious. She'd received a cryptic message the same day as the town meeting, only hours before her SUV had burst into flames.

He turned the envelope over in his hand and scrutinized it further. "No return address?"

"And no signature."

"Did you see who delivered it?"

"No. The staff had already left so I didn't get a chance to ask them either."

"Someone must have dropped it off in person?"

"Or put it in the mailbox outside the school."

Riggs considered the possibilities. "Meaning it could have been a student or anyone in town."

Kate ran a hand through her hair again. Dammit, he wished she'd quit touching it. The urge to replace her fingers with his own grabbed him once more. To see if her hair was as silky as it looked.

"I guess it could have been a current student, although I can't think of anyone I've had serious trouble with this year," Kate said. "Besides, the message implies whoever sent it blames me for the shooting, which suggests it's a former student or a family member of one."

Riggs tossed back the remainder of his whiskey then leaned forward, hands on his knees. "The shooting wasn't your fault, Kate. Ned was a troubled teenager."

Emotions clouded Kate's face. "But it *was* my fault," she said, her voice quivering.

Riggs didn't believe that for a minute, but obviously Kate did. "Why would you say that?"

Kate dropped her head into her hands and squeezed her eyes closed. She looked so tormented that he wanted to wrap his arms around her and comfort her.

But he clenched his hands by his sides and forced himself not to reach for her.

SHAME FILLED KATE, mingling with the guilt that had dogged her for years. She'd kept quiet about her part in Ned's breakdown. If Riggs knew her secret, he might hate her.

She'd give anything to be able to go back and re-write time.

"Kate, talk to me."

The tenderness in his voice almost undid her. But she'd held in the truth for so long that it was time to break her silence. "I turned Ned down when he asked me to the school dance," she admitted. "I…didn't think anything about it at the time. I was shy and worried about my Trig exam, and… I rejected him without considering his feelings."

Riggs scrubbed a hand down his face. "Turning a

guy down for a date is no reason for him to go crazy and shoot up the school, Kate. Ned had emotional problems."

"I know. Kids bullied him and teased him, but I didn't do anything about it. Didn't stand up for him."

"You weren't personally responsible for him or anyone else except yourself," Riggs said.

Tears glistened in Kate's eyes. "But Billy said my rejection sent Ned over the edge."

Anger flashed across Riggs's face. "Billy Hodgkins is a bully. Always was. Always will be."

Kate had never liked Billy, either. He'd pick fights with guys and tried to cop a feel with girls when no one was looking.

But he'd lost his brother because of her, and she understood why he hated her.

"When did Billy tell you this?" Riggs asked.

"At Mom's funeral." Kate massaged her temple as the painful memory resurfaced. The day she'd buried her mother was a rainy day. The wind had blown leaves and silk flowers across the cemetery while half the residents and students stood sniffling and crying beneath black umbrellas. Others were at the hospital with their children who'd been injured. Brynn had been undergoing surgery.

And Macy…? She'd needed her friend, but she'd deserted Kate.

"What else did Billy say, Kate?"

"That Ned had a huge crush on me, and it took him weeks to get up his nerve to ask me out. When I blew him off, it broke him."

She swallowed hard. "If I'd agreed to go to the dance with him, maybe he wouldn't have brought that gun to school and murdered our classmates and my mother." She wrung her hands together. Her nails were clipped short to keep her from biting them, but she had a habit of rubbing her fingers together when she was nervous. She was absentmindedly doing that now.

Riggs's hand covered hers, stilling her jittery movements. "Look at me, Kate."

She shook her head. It was difficult enough to face herself in the mirror, much less look at the town hero.

"Kate. Look. At. Me." His firm but tender voice made her glance up, and she swallowed hard.

"School shootings are a complex problem. If you're to blame, then so am I, and every other kid at school who ever ignored Ned. So are the teachers and society and social media," Riggs said firmly.

Amy had said the same thing. Still, Kate wished she'd been nicer to Ned.

Riggs wrapped her hands in his, rubbing them. "If Billy is still bitter and blames you, he might have sent that note to spook you."

Riggs released her hands and stood. "I'll call Stone in the morning and ask him to have a talk with Billy."

Kate stood, although she was reluctant for him to leave. She'd lived alone for years, but the letter of blame and car fire disturbed her, and she suddenly didn't want to be alone.

"Get that security system set up tomorrow," he reminded her.

Emotions welled in her throat. "I will. I also need to

call my insurance company about the repairs and arrange for a rental car."

He carried his glass to the kitchen and set it on the counter, then walked to the door. She followed, torn between pushing him out the door and asking him to stay. He filled her doorway with his massive shoulders and big body.

Lord help her, he oozed sex appeal. Afraid he could read her mind, she dragged her gaze away from him and folded her arms across her chest.

"Thanks for driving me home."

"Of course." He paused at the door. "Remember what I said, Kate. The shooting wasn't your fault, so don't let that damn note get to you."

She gave a little nod, although telling herself that and believing it were two different things.

"You need to show it to Stone," Riggs said. "Maybe he can lift some prints from it, or have the handwriting analyzed."

"I'll drop it by his office tomorrow."

"I can do it if you want," Riggs offered. "I want to talk to him about your car anyway." His brow furrowed. "Or maybe I can pick you up, and we can go together. I'll drive you over to pick up that rental car, too."

Kate stiffened. "I don't want to impose on you. You've already done enough."

His eyes flashed with irritation. "I have a couple of days off and don't mind driving you," he said. "I want to make sure you're safe, Kate."

She wanted to ask why he cared. They weren't even

friends. But she clamped her mouth shut. Riggs was not only a fireman, he also worked arson investigation.

Maybe he suspected the fire wasn't accidental.

He removed a card from his pocket and laid it on the table by the door. "My phone number—cell and work. Call me if you need anything."

She needed him to stay. To hold her tonight and help her forget that she could have died in that fire.

To help her forget that someone might hate her enough to want her dead.

Get a grip, Kate. You have to stand on your own.

So she said good-night and watched him leave. As his vehicle disappeared down the drive, she locked and bolted the door and walked back to the living room.

Odd, but the big club chair looked empty without Riggs in it.

Silently chastising herself for falling prey to his charm, she rinsed her mug, stowed it and his glass in the dishwasher.

She checked the sliding-glass doors to make sure they were locked then stepped into her bedroom.

The scent of Riggs's masculine aftershave lingered from when he'd searched her house. She wondered what he'd thought about her furnishings.

Stupid. Riggs Benford was not the kind of man who noticed a woman's furniture. He was a player.

And she didn't intend to be played. Even if he was interested—which he was not.

She changed into a tank top and pajama pants, then folded down her thick purple comforter. An image of Riggs stretched out naked on her bed taunted her.

He would look ridiculous against the plush bedding. But her bed would be so much cozier with his sexy body in it.

She punched her pillow. She had to banish those kinds of thoughts. She wanted more than one night with a man.

And Riggs wasn't the commitment type.

A noise outside jarred her and she startled. The wind? Thunder?

Nerves on edge, she hurried to the sliding-glass doors, opened them, then stepped onto her screened porch and looked out into the night. Lighting zigzagged across the tops of the pines and oaks, sharp jolts of light against the jagged ridges of Bear Mountain and the dark, inky night.

Then a movement.

Fear slithered through her. Someone was in the woods behind her house…

DAMN. DAMN. DAMN.

He watched Kate McKendrick through the window of her bedroom with a mixture of hate and disappointment.

She had made it out of the car alive. She should have died.

Then maybe all this talk about tearing down the old school would stop.

He'd lit a joint and taken a drag as he'd watched that firefighter drive away.

Riggs Benford. Arson investigator. Town hero.

He could be a problem. But he couldn't save Kate.

Not if she kept moving ahead with the dedication and reunion.

All the classmates who'd left town were coming back now. He'd heard them at the diner, the coffee shop, everywhere he went in town. They were already gathering and reminiscing. Talking about the good old days.

And the bad one. The one that had ripped apart friends and families and put some of them in the ground.

His life was bad enough. That was the *last* thing he needed.

For folks to remember. Then they might figure out who he was.

He'd blow all of them to pieces before he allowed that to happen.

Chapter Five

The next morning, Riggs rubbed his bleary eyes as he poured his second cup of coffee. He'd barely slept all night for worrying about Kate.

He took a long, slow sniff, grateful for the burst of caffeine in the rich scent of the dark roast blend, then carried it to his back deck and studied the sharp angles and slopes of the mountain ridges.

Kate was right. Briar Ridge had once been a hopping, happy town. He'd grown up enjoying hiking, whitewater rafting, and skiing. Before his mother had had enough of his daddy, she'd sewn handmade quilts to sell at the festivals, and canned jams and jellies for the local mercantile. His father had made fun of her, but tourists had loved the homemade goodies. Kids had flocked to the souvenir section that was complete with stuffed bears, T-shirts with images of Bear Mountain, and crystals from the old mines.

Kate wanted to restore that happy atmosphere.

He swallowed hard. God, Kate.

The frightened look on her face as she'd stood watching her SUV erupt into flames had haunted him in his sleep. Then the pain and guilt when she'd confessed about her conversation with Billy Hodgkins at her mother's funeral.

If Billy hurt Kate, he'd… Do what? Kill him?

He'd never thought of himself as a violent man. He *saved* lives.

But…something about Kate had gotten under his skin last night and triggered his protective instincts.

Hell, not a one of his classmates would probably believe that. In high school, Kate hadn't been his type. On the surface, he'd liked to flirt and date around, anything to feed his ego after his old man had beaten him down.

But he'd never thought about being serious. Hadn't really thought he deserved a good girl like Kate.

Kate was…real. Beautiful, but not a made-up doll who focused on her looks or spending three hundred dollars on a pair of designer shoes.

Oh, yeah, he'd dated a woman, more than one, who'd fit that description.

His sexual prowess and the dangerous side of his job drew them like flies to honey. They thought he was exciting, brave, some kind of superhero for running into burning buildings when everyone else was running the other way.

He was no damn hero. He just did what he could to save others because…because he'd watched friends and classmates die and had been helpless to save them.

Sex was one thing.

Commitment was another.

So far, he hadn't found any woman who made him consider the Big C.

But the bookworm girl who'd hidden behind big square glasses fifteen years ago was smart, cared about people, and had stood up to half the town the night before for something she believed in. She wanted to make a difference in the world and fought for it.

She's not interested in you, buddy.

His phone buzzed with a text from Stone.

Should have the report from the mechanic on Kate's car by nine.

He sent a return text.

Will meet you at ten. Need to talk.

Copy that. My office. Ten o'clock.

Speaking of the devilish woman who'd kept him up all night, his phone buzzed. Kate.

He punched Connect. "Morning," he said through gritted teeth. Damn. His voice was gravelly from loss of sleep. Had his greeting sounded like a come-on?

"It's Kate," she said a little stiffly. "I need to set up a time for the security installation. What time will you be here?"

Ah, yeah. Back to Kate's safety and the reason—excuse—he'd used to see her today. "I told Stone we'd meet him at his office at ten."

"Okay, I'll be ready." Her breath rattled over the line. "Or if you have other things to do, I can Uber."

She almost sounded hopeful that he'd retract his

offer. But if Kate was in danger, she didn't need to get in a car with a stranger. "No. Like I said, it's my day off. Why don't we grab breakfast first?" So he was a glutton for punishment.

Silence for a second. "Thanks, but I've already eaten. I just need time to shower and get dressed."

He closed his eyes and fought a groan as she disconnected. Images of Kate naked and stepping beneath the shower water made his body harden. For a brief second, he imagined her luscious curves and full breasts dotted with water, her pink lips parted for his tongue to dive inside for a taste.

But the sound of the wind beating at the windowpane jarred him back to reality and he cursed himself. Kate McKendrick did not want him. She never had.

He would simply offer his assistance in keeping her safe because firefighters vowed to protect the public. Nothing more.

Kate was a settle-down type of woman. After all she'd suffered, she deserved some happiness.

And a man who'd fulfill her dreams.

He was not that man.

THE EARLY MORNING sunlight forced Kate to look at herself realistically in the mirror. Dark circles marred the skin beneath her eyes, and her face looked…tired. After she'd seen that movement behind her house the night before, she'd studied the woods and darkness for an hour. But no one had surfaced.

She'd finally reconciled that the shadow belonged to a deer, and she'd crawled into bed.

But she'd lain awake listening for sounds of an intruder half the night.

When she'd finally fallen asleep, she'd been running for her life. Billy Hodgkins was chasing her through the woods with a butcher knife. "You'll pay for killing my brother!" he shouted. "It was all your fault."

She'd woken and realized she was alone. Safe from Billy. In her own bed, not in the woods. She'd tossed and turned for another hour, then finally drifted back to sleep only to dream of Riggs in her bed.

Riggs with his sultry eyes raking over her bare skin. His hands and lips following, stirring desires every place he touched…

She'd bolted awake again, her body humming with need.

But the face in the mirror gave her clarity. Hers was not the face of a woman Riggs would be lusting for. Besides, how could she be attracted to a man who flirted with every woman he met? With a man who'd abandoned his child?

Granted, Riggs had been seventeen when he'd gotten Cassidy pregnant, but his son lived in the same town and attended Briar Ridge High, and Riggs had nothing to do with him.

Focusing on that thought sobered her and she moved away from the mirror. She phoned her insurance agent and then the rental car company and arranged to pick up a red Ford Escape by noon.

A knock sounded, and through the front window she spotted Riggs's black truck in her drive. She grabbed her purse and rushed to the door, deciding she didn't need Riggs invading her space this morning. His scent and image in that club chair was torture enough.

When she opened the door, he stood towering in front of her, his big masculine body exuding sexuality. Morning sunlight fought through the dark clouds outside, highlighting the caramel streaking his thick dark hair and bronzed skin. His dimple appeared as he greeted her with one of his killer smiles.

"Morning, Kate."

"Hi." She dragged her gaze from his face, which was a mistake because her height put her at his shoulders, forcing her to look at muscles straining the confines of a black T-shirt emblazoned with the logo for the Briar Ridge fire department on the front. A silver-studded belt buckle circled his waist where a tight pair of jeans hugged his muscular hips and thighs.

Dear Lord, the man was built. His forearms looked like tree trunks. He must lift weights...

Could he lift her?

Heat crept up her neck at the unbidden thought and she inhaled sharply to calm her raging hormones.

"Are you ready?" he asked.

She didn't trust her voice to speak, so she simply nodded, stepped onto the porch and locked the door.

"Did you arrange for the security system installation?" he asked as they settled in his truck.

"Yes, they're coming this afternoon."

There, small talk was good.

Except she couldn't think of anything else to say.

He cut his eyes toward her as he started the engine. "Did you sleep okay?"

No, I dreamed of Billy chasing me and then you in my bed. "Not great," she admitted.

"Sorry." Riggs backed from the drive and turned onto the road. An awkward silence fell between them as he drove toward town. Fanny's Five & Dime store looked just like it had years ago, except now the merchandise consisted of dollar items and it had been renamed accordingly. The Cut and Dye was hustling with business as usual, and mothers and fathers were already strolling babies to the park. Other early morning joggers and walkers occupied the running trail, and the parking lot for the breakfast spot, The Bear Claw, was full.

Five minutes later, they reached the sheriff's office, a two-story, rustic brick building with a wrought-iron railing. Riggs parked and rushed around the front of the truck to open her door. Polite.

Kate climbed out before he reached the passenger side.

He quirked a thick dark brow as if in challenge. "Next time I'll get the door."

Next time? "In case you haven't noticed, Riggs, I'm not some delicate little flower." *Like the women you date.*

A tiny smile tugged at his lips. "Just using my manners."

Her heart fluttered. Of course he was. It didn't mean anything personal. And, for heaven's sake, why had she drawn attention to her size?

He raked his eyes over her, making her body tingle from his perusal. Unnerved, she rushed up the steps to escape further comment.

They reached the door to the building at the same time, and Riggs wrapped his long fingers around the door handle. "Now, Kate, I'm going to open the door for you, so say 'thank you.'"

She expected to see laughter in his expression, but his smoky eyes were locked on her face. Serious. Waiting. Challenging her.

"Thank you." She bit out the word then practically jogged inside when he opened it. Irritation at herself needled her. Good grief, she wasn't usually rude to people. But Riggs elicited feelings and thoughts she didn't know how to handle.

The receptionist, Bobbie Jean, a middle-aged woman with a short perm, smiled a greeting as they entered. Stone glanced up from a front desk when they entered, one hand gripping the phone. When he saw them, he ended the call, stood and circled the desk, and offered them a coffee.

Nerves bunched Kate's stomach, so she declined. Riggs muttered a comment about needing all the caffeine he could get and accepted a cup.

Stone spoke to his receptionist. "We'll be in my office if you need me."

Bobbie Jean gave a nod, and Kate and Riggs followed Stone through a swinging door down a hallway. A sign to the left read H*olding Cell*. Two rooms labeled Interrogation Rooms 1 and 2 respectively were opposite it. Beyond those, they stepped into a small private office. A photograph of Stone's father, the former sheriff, hung over the desk with a commendation he'd received from the mayor for his quick response to the school shooting.

Kate sank into a metal chair, noting more pictures of his father hanging on the wall behind the desk. The resemblance between Stone and his father was strong although Stone held a seriousness to his eyes that hadn't been there before the shooting.

The sheriff had visited her after the massacre, but she'd been too traumatized and grief stricken to help. He'd questioned everyone in town, though, determined to find out if Ned had an accomplice.

Unfortunately everyone was either in shock or wasn't talking. And no answer ever came.

Stone and Riggs were about the same height, only Stone's hair was a little shaggy and unkempt, and his eyes hazel. He was handsome, but much more serious than Riggs had ever been. She was surprised Stone was still single, but his brother had been blinded in the shooting, and Stone seemed married to the job. When he'd become sheriff, he'd vowed to one day find out if Ned had acted alone. Once he did, that person would pay.

"I talked to the mechanic about your car," Stone said.

Kate twisted her hands together. "And?"

"Someone cut your gas line, which caused a leak," Stone said.

Kate's pulse hammered. Her gas line had been cut… Intentionally. Not an accident.

Dear God. Someone *had* tried to kill her.

ANGER SHOT THROUGH RIGGS. He'd had a bad feeling about that fire.

Kate's breath rushed out. "I know some people are

upset about the new school, but I can't imagine anyone in town trying to kill me because of it."

Riggs squeezed her shoulder. "Tell him about Billy."

Kate clenched her purse strap. "It was a long time ago. I don't want to cast stones at an innocent person."

"Tell him," Riggs said through gritted teeth.

"Please," Stone said quietly. "No matter how insignificant you might think something is, it could be helpful."

Kate forced a neutral tone as she described her confrontation with Billy at her mother's funeral. Sharing the hurtful words was difficult, but she refused to fall apart in front of these two strong men. Or to remain a prisoner of the past.

"Kate, he was wrong to blame you, and you know it," Stone said. "My father investigated the Hodgkins family. The parents were…questionable. Billy was as hard on his brother as the rest of the kids at school or worse. His mother said Billy used to play mean tricks on Ned. More than once, he tied Ned to the doghouse out back and forced him to sleep in it when they were gone."

Kate shivered. Riggs hadn't heard that before, either, but it confirmed his opinion of Billy Hodgkins.

"I'm surprised Ned didn't turn the gun on his brother," Riggs muttered.

Stone shrugged. "I guess blood is thicker than water. Ned was troubled and unleashed it on all of us at school instead."

"Some of our classmates did tease him," Kate said. "And I did reject him."

Riggs huffed, unsympathetic. "If I went off and shot

up people every time I got rejected, I'd be in prison for life."

Kate's eyes widened, but she didn't comment.

"Have you seen or spoken to Billy lately?" Stone asked.

Kate shook her head. "Not really. After that day, I avoided him."

"We both know he was at the meeting," Stone said.

"He cornered her outside behind the town hall," Riggs interjected.

"Kate?" Stone arched a brow toward her. "Did he threaten you?"

"He mumbled something, but I didn't understand him, then he ran off when he saw Riggs."

Stone drummed his fingers on his desk. "When I asked Billy why he was at the meeting, he said he wanted to talk to you in private, Kate. I told him to calm down, that that wasn't going to happen."

Riggs angled his head toward Kate. "Did you bring the note?"

Stone leaned back in his chair, hands linked behind his head. "What note?"

Kate removed the invitation from her purse and offered it to Stone. "I received this yesterday in the school mail, but I have no idea who sent it."

Stone rocked forward in his chair, took the envelope and examined it, as Riggs had done. "No return address?"

"No, it was in with my mail at school. Anyone could have dropped it in our outside mailbox without being noticed."

"All the publicity about the new school may have triggered traumatic memories for Billy and his family, and he lashed out at you, Kate," Riggs suggested.

"I'll send this to the lab for analysis." Stone put the invitation card back in the envelope and placed it in an evidence bag. "I also had a crime team go over your SUV, Kate. The fire will make it difficult, but hopefully we'll get some forensics from the vehicle."

"Are you going to question Billy?" Riggs asked.

Stone nodded. "As soon as we finish here, I'll look for him. And I'll find out where his parents are. It's possible they may be upset about the publicity." He gestured to the front-page article in the morning paper.

A photograph of Kate at the podium in front of the town appeared above the headline *Principal Kate McKendrick Pushes for Demolition of Infamous Briar Ridge High Where a Tragic Mass Murder Occurred Fifteen Years Ago.*

Kate stared at the cutline. *Locals in An Uproar... Did One of Them Threaten Kate McKendrick?*

The article also featured photographs of the bloody scene, the rescue workers, then Ned and his family.

Stone grunted. "That damn Gretta Wright likes to keep things stirred up. She was on the morning news with the story."

"If Ned's parents saw the publicity, I'm sure they're upset," Kate said. "They went through hell after the shooting. People practically ran them out of town."

"True, but my dad suspected they were holding something back," Stone said. "Only he never figured out what." He patted his holster. "Meanwhile, Kate, I'll assign a deputy to guard you twenty-four-seven."

Kate shook her head. "That's not necessary, Stone, I'll be fine."

Riggs gritted his teeth. He wasn't surprised Kate declined protection. She was stubborn and independent.

But she was also in danger.

And he'd be damned if he'd sit by and let anyone hurt her.

Chapter Six

The idea of a bodyguard hovering around her day and night made Kate feel claustrophobic. She was a private person. Led a boring life.

All she'd wanted to do was to help others heal the way she was starting to heal.

"Come on," Riggs said. "I'll drive you over to pick up that rental car."

"Thanks. But I'll walk. I need the exercise."

"Kate, you're not walking three miles to pick up a car when I can drive you, especially under the circumstances." Irritation tinged his voice, so she clamped her teeth together and refrained from a retort.

Why was he being so insistent? "Fine. Then you've done your duty, Riggs."

He paused on the front stoop of the sheriff's office, a frown creasing his brows. "I'm sorry you find my company so repulsive."

Kate squeezed her eyes shut for a moment, chastising herself for being rude. "I didn't mean it like that," she said as she looked up at him. "I appreciate your time and concern. But I don't want to be a burden."

A wry laugh rumbled from his chest. "You are not a burden, Kate. Prickly, but not a burden." His voice turned gruff. "And like it or not, I'm going to stick around and make sure no one hurts you."

She gaped at him as if he'd grown a second head. "That's not necessary. I can take care of myself. And I'm sure you have other friends to meet up with."

"No," he said bluntly. "No plans today."

"Good grief, Riggs. Don't you have a girlfriend waiting?"

He shook his head. "Not that I know of."

"That's right, you have *several*," she said, injecting a teasing tone to her voice. Or was it a hint of jealousy? "I'd hate to upset one of them."

He pressed his lips together in a thin line. "I get it. You think I'm a womanizer. But high school was a long damn time ago, Kate. People change."

She stared at him again, as if she didn't know whether to believe him or to call him a liar.

His chest thundered.

"Let's just get the rental car," she finally said. "I have to drop by the school afterward and pick up some year-end paperwork."

"Fine." He squared his shoulders and started down the steps, jaw clenched.

Lord help her. She had the insane sense she'd hurt his feelings.

But why would he be hurt? He might have changed, but he was Riggs Benford, a poster boy for bachelorhood.

And she wanted a real relationship. A husband and kids one day.

Get hold of yourself, Kate. He's simply giving you a ride.

Although old hurts rose to taunt her. Tony, a popular basketball star in school, had taken her to a movie one night. Later, he'd left her on the side of the road. His words had been like a stake in her heart. *Big girls like you need to learn to put out. That's the only way you'll have a boyfriend.*

Worse, he'd lied and bragged to the other guys on the team that she had.

Jerk.

That incident had taught her a lesson. She couldn't trust players. They used you for sex then bragged about it. She didn't intend to be the butt of anyone's joke, not ever again.

So, in college, she'd kept her nose in her books. Earning her education and becoming a teacher had meant everything to her. She'd wanted to honor her mother and be a mentor to kids the same way she had.

They climbed into his pickup and rode in silence to the rental car office. "Thanks, Riggs." She forced a polite smile. "It was very nice of you to give me a lift."

His chiseled jaw tightened even more, emotions glittering in his eyes. "I'll follow you to school and make sure it's safe."

"Thanks, but again, not necessary. A few teachers are there today, packing up, and the custodian is organizing and boxing up furniture to ship to the new facility. Besides, no one is going to try to hurt me at school during the day."

His look suggested he wasn't convinced, but she'd

obviously hammered home the fact that she didn't want him around. Except, he wasn't repulsive at all and she liked having him around. That was the problem.

But Kate was a practical kind of girl. No use fantasizing about things she couldn't have.

"Kate." He caught her arm before she could escape. "I'm serious. Be careful. And call me if you need anything."

Kate stared at his wide, blunt fingers for a moment, her skin tingling from his touch.

Afraid Riggs would read her reaction to him, she slid from the truck and forced herself not to look back as she hurried up to the rental car office.

Her phone buzzed as she entered. Gretta Wright.

Kate hissed between her teeth. She despised the woman. Gretta's high school gossip rag had fed on any juicy tidbit she could dig up on the students.

Her face stung at the memory of the humiliating picture Gretta had posted of Kate in her gym clothes. Gym clothes that were too tight because someone had switched her uniform with a smaller one as a prank. Her gym shorts had ripped when she'd run hurdles on the track.

Riggs and the entire soccer team had been watching. Laughing.

Cheeks flushing from the memory, she ignored the call and finished the paperwork for the rental car, then snagged the keys to the Escape. When she was safe inside, she checked her voice mail.

"Kate, it's Gretta. I'd like to interview you about the meeting last night, and about your accident. I'll meet you or come by your house if you'd rather, whichever you prefer."

Kate deleted the message. She did not intend to share her fears about the car fire with a reporter, especially Gretta Wright.

KATE'S ALOOF MANNER toward him bothered Riggs as he drove back to the police station. Dammit.

Kate was nice to everyone. Except him.

Because she thought he jumped from one woman's bed to another, and that he was a deadbeat dad.

Well, hell, at one time, he'd been a commitaphobe. But that was a long damn time ago. The shooting, his physical therapy, witnessing others' pain…it had changed him. He used to enjoy a hot night between the sheets. He'd disappear out the door as soon as his lover fell asleep and go home to his own bed where no one demanded anything of him.

But lately the fun had turned to boredom. His bachelor ways, waking up at home alone, had become… lonely.

Maybe he had been a jerk to women. But he never would have abandoned his kid. *Never.*

He knew what it was like to have a father who didn't care.

He parked at the sheriff's office and rushed inside, hoping to catch Stone.

His friend clipped his phone on his belt as Riggs entered his private office.

"Forget something?" Stone asked.

"I wanted to talk about Kate."

Stone pivoted in his rolling chair and raised a brow. "What's up with you and her anyway?"

"Nothing." Riggs jammed his hands in his pockets. "But after the climate of the meeting, I'm worried. Did you find Billy?"

Stone tapped his foot. "Not yet. I was just on the phone with Celeste at the inn. Billy isn't on the guest list."

"Then where the hell is he staying?"

Stone shrugged. "Don't know yet. Do you remember who he was friends with back in the day?"

Riggs struggled to recall. He and Billy had run in different circles.

Stone pulled a yearbook from the shelf above his desk. Riggs looked over his shoulder as Stone thumbed through their class roster.

"Woody Mathis," Stone said. "He and Billy were buddies."

"That's right," Riggs said. "Woody was injured in the shooting."

"Yes, he was," Stone said.

"Did Woody have family?" Riggs asked.

"Just his daddy, but he was mean and a gambler. Died a year after Woody was hurt. Heard the house went into foreclosure. Not sure what happened to Woody. Haven't seen him around."

"I heard he got hooked on painkillers," Riggs said.

"Sounds about right." Stone grunted.

"What about the Hodgkins's old house?"

"That's a place to start. There's also the old lodge outside of town."

"It shut down two years ago," Riggs said.

"The very reason it would make a good place to hide if someone didn't want his or her whereabouts known."

True.

"Problem is, Billy isn't the only one upset about tearing down the old school," Stone said. "Any one of the victims or their loved ones could be responsible for that note, and the attempt on Kate's life."

"That's a lot of suspects. How can I help?" Riggs asked.

Stone crossed his arms. "This is police work, Riggs. Let me do my job."

"Two heads are better than one," Riggs argued.

"Don't you need to be at work?" Stone asked.

Riggs shrugged. "I have a couple of days off. You know how our shifts run. Three days on. Three off."

"Right." Stone drummed his fingers on his desk. "My deputy can start looking into the alumni, and Macy Stark is in town for the reunion. She's with the FBI and on leave because of an injury. I thought we could use a fresh pair of eyes and want her to review Dad's reports for anything that might stand out about the case. Maybe she'll find a clue pointing to an accomplice."

Riggs thought back. The school counselor, Amy Turner, might know. She was serving on the committee with Kate to create the new memorial. "Did Ms. Turner offer insight as to who she thought might have helped Ned?"

"No. According to Dad's notes, she was determined to protect her students' confidence. But I'll talk to her. Maybe after all this time, she'll change her mind."

"What can I do to help?" Riggs asked again.

A smile teased Stone's eyes. "Keep an eye on Kate for a couple of days. Not in an official capacity, of course, but just as a friend."

Kate wouldn't be happy about that. And she obviously didn't consider him a friend.

His gut tightened. He'd do it anyway. Even if he couldn't charm her into liking him, he could keep her safe. If for no other reason than to finally uncover the truth about Ned's possible accomplice.

Stone stood, adjusting his holster. "I'll ask my deputy to check out the Hodgkins's old homestead. I'm going to take a look around that abandoned lodge."

"I'll go with you," Riggs offered.

Stone gestured to the door. "All right. But follow my lead. If Billy is at the lodge and appears to be dangerous, you have to stay in the car."

"Of course." Riggs forced an even keel to his tone. He'd let Stone take the lead.

But if he learned Billy was behind that note or the attempt on Kate's life, he couldn't promise he wouldn't beat the hell out of him before Stone carted him off to jail.

KATE HAD THE eerie sense someone was watching her as she drove from the rental car office toward the high school. Her stomach growled, a reminder she'd lied about eating breakfast because she'd been too nervous about seeing Riggs again to eat.

She pulled into Pearl's Dine & Pie, parked and glanced around at the red-and-white sign lettering above the metal-embossed image of a red thunderbird. Locals and visitors packed the place, enjoying a late breakfast and chatting over coffee and Pearl's famous cobblers. With school out for the summer, a few teens wandered in, still wearing pajamas, to soak up the blueberry pancakes and lattes.

The parking lot at the inn next door also had more cars than she'd seen in a decade. Most probably belonging to former classmates and alumni. Some of whom had been at the meeting the night before.

Any one of them could have sent her that message.

She checked over her shoulder and scanned the parking lot before she slid from the car. Thankfully, Billy wasn't lurking around.

Mrs. Gaines's silver BMW was parked in the lot. Kate made to leave but decided she couldn't run from everyone opposed to the demolition of the old school.

She ached to reconcile with Brynn, too, only guilt held her back. Brynn was paralyzed because Ned had gone ballistic. Maybe there had been other factors, but she'd definitely contributed with her callous rejection.

How could Brynn possibly forgive her when she was confined to a wheelchair?

Mrs. Gaines had never approved of Kate and had wanted Brynn to socialize with the more elite crowd, as if Kate and her mother weren't good enough. After the accident, she'd cut Kate completely off from seeing Brynn.

Brynn had been groomed for Miss Teen Briar Ridge since the age of five, her mother traipsing her through competition after competition across the state. Her mother insisted on perfection and had been critical of Brynn if every hair wasn't in place. She also demanded perfection in herself and her daughter, an exhausting task.

Was she still critical or had she softened with Brynn's injury?

Kate walked up to the entrance. As soon as she opened the door, the heavenly scent of sausage and gravy wafted around her.

Instead of a sweet tooth, Kate liked hearty food—a biscuit with bacon, sausage, or country fried ham. Mrs. Gaines had once commented that Kate ate like a man.

Her own mother had scoffed at the comment and told Kate to eat whatever her body craved. That protein built muscles, and confidence built character.

Silence stretched across the crowded noisy room as she entered. Kate lifted her chin then crossed to the counter. Some patrons offered a tentative smile while others pierced her with angry looks.

As she seated herself on a stool, Pearl pushed a cup of coffee toward her. "Here you go, sweetie. You want the usual?"

"Yes, to go. Thanks."

Pearl patted her hand. "For the record, I believe in what you're doing. It's high time someone shook this town back to life again."

Kate murmured thanks again, rifling through her purse to pay as the silence giving way to whispers. On their way out, three people stopped to say they supported her.

She sipped her coffee, her senses on edge as footsteps sounded behind her. "Kate?"

She froze, bracing herself for the wrath of the mayor's wife as she pivoted. "Hi, Mrs. Gaines." Brynn sat beside her mother, hands clenched around the arms of her chair, worrying her lower lip with her teeth. Her silky blond hair fell across her shoulders in loose waves, and she wore a pale pink blouse that highlighted her perfect ivory skin.

Brynn was the most beautiful girl Kate had ever known and a tender heart who loved animals. Losing her friendship had carved an empty hole in Kate's already shattered heart. Then again, if the school signified a new beginning, maybe she could start over with Brynn.

"Brynn," she said with a hopeful smile, "it's nice to see you."

Mrs. Gaines stepped in front of Brynn. "I've changed my mind. I think building a new school will benefit this town and the people in it."

Kate narrowed her eyes. The edge to the woman's tone and the sudden tightening of Brynn's face suggested Brynn's mother had her own agenda. Appearances were everything to the haughty woman.

"Thank you," Kate said. "I appreciate your support."

Brynn wheeled her chair away from her mother, an indication something was wrong. "Is it true someone sabotaged your car, Kate?" Brynn asked.

Kate's stomach clenched. "That's what the sheriff said."

Fear darkened Brynn's beautiful blue eyes. "Do they know who did it?"

"Not yet. But Stone is investigating."

Mrs. Gaines snapped her fingers. "We have to go, Brynn. Your therapy session, remember?"

A pained look flashed across Brynn's face before she gestured at her chair. "No, Mother, how could I forget when you constantly remind me?"

Disapproval flared in Mrs. Gaines's eyes at Brynn's tone then she threw up a hand, dismissing Kate.

Brynn looked contrite, as if she wanted to say more as she wheeled herself out the door.

Just as Pearl brought Kate's to-go order, Amy Turner came in. When she spotted Kate, she hurried over to her. Worry filled her green eyes and she looked upset. Before she took a seat, her eyes darted around the diner as if she was nervous.

"Kate, is it true what they said on the news?" Amy whispered. "Did someone threaten you?"

Kate lowered her voice. "Yes. And my car was tampered with. But I don't know who did it yet." Kate shifted. "How did you know about the threat?"

"It's all over town, and I saw Gretta on the news," Amy said. "People are saying it has to do with the shooting."

Kate licked her suddenly dry lips. "Someone doesn't want the past dredged up. Amy, I know you maintain strict student/therapist confidentiality, but the threats rouse suspicion that Ned did have an accomplice. And that that person doesn't want the truth exposed."

Amy's face paled. "I…don't know what to say, Kate. If I'd known Ned had an accomplice, I'd have spoken up."

Kate studied her friend. "Maybe you can think about it, look back at your old files to see if anything sticks out now that you might have missed then."

Amy nodded, but her phone was buzzing in her purse, and she reached for it. "I will." She squeezed Kate's arm, her eyes darkening with worry. "Be careful, Kate. If Ned did have an accomplice and he got off for fifteen years, he's not going to want to go to jail now."

Kate nodded, her stomach in her throat as she snatched her food and headed out to her car.

Chapter Seven

Riggs skimmed the list of classmates staying at the inn while Stone drove, scrutinizing each name as a potential suspect. He tried to place faces with those who'd attended the meeting the night before, but over the years, classmates had aged and changed in appearance.

Stone parked in front of the abandoned lodge, which was set off the road on a scenic ridge near the top of Bear Mountain. The place had once catered to hunters and fishermen in the summers and skiers in the winter.

A rusted black pickup was parked to the side, beneath a sagging carport with a metal roof. The paint on the wood lodge walls was chipped and muddy, the windows cracked, the awning on the front hanging askew as if a storm had ripped it from the roof.

"Stay here," Stone told him. "If Billy's inside, he might be armed."

Riggs grunted. "I'll back you up."

Stone gave him a stern look. "Keep behind me and be a lookout. I don't want you getting shot on my watch."

"Can't say as I'd like that, either," Riggs said with a wry chuckle.

Stone gripped his service revolver as he climbed from the police car.

As Riggs approached the deserted run-down building, he wished he had a damn gun. But carrying a weapon seemed counterintuitive to his job.

Riggs scanned the front of the building for signs someone was around. A curtain slid to the side in the room on the end. "Last room," he told Stone.

Stone lowered his gun to his side but held it at the ready. Together they strode up to the door, and Stone knocked. "Sheriff Lawson, open up!"

A screeching noise erupted from the rear. Then a window opened and a man crawled through it.

"He's running," Riggs yelled to Stone. "Side window."

Stone signaled Riggs to stay back and then eased toward the right. Riggs inched down the steps and darted behind a live oak flanking the driveway. The man dropped to the ground, hunched like a wild animal about to pounce.

Not Billy. But Billy's old buddy, Woody Mathis. Dressed in tattered clothing and muddy boots, with several days of beard growth on his face, he looked as if he hadn't seen a shower or a hot meal in days. His eyes appeared glassy, glazed over from drug use.

"Stop!" Stone shouted.

Woody hesitated then cursed and aimed his gun at Stone.

"Put it down, Woody," Stone ordered.

"I didn't do anything wrong." Woody darted for the woods behind the lodge. But he must have decided escaping on foot was futile, so he turned and dashed toward the pickup.

Riggs couldn't let him escape. Stone crept forward, gun still braced, but Woody pivoted and fired a shot. His hand unsteady, the bullet hit the dirt at Stone's feet.

Stone threw up a warning hand. "Woody, don't do this."

Woody shouted a curse and reached for the pickup's door handle. He obviously didn't intend to turn himself in.

With Woody focused on Stone, Riggs took advantage, left the cover of the oak and jumped Woody from behind, knocking his gun to the ground.

An image of Kate's face haunted him as Riggs slammed Woody up against the truck and jerked his arms behind him. "Did you mess with Kate McKendrick's car?"

Stone jogged up to them, pulled his handcuffs from his belt and gestured for Riggs to let him handle the situation.

Instead, Riggs tightened his hold. He wanted answers. "Did you?"

"I told you I didn't do nothing," Woody said in a shaky voice.

"Then why the hell did you run?" Riggs growled.

RIGGS'S REMINDER ABOUT the security system taunted Kate as she parked at the school. She'd felt safe in her new house until that note and the fire. Now, she wondered if she was being stalked. Watched at school and at home.

The redbrick school, built in the fifties, had served

the community for decades. Classrooms were held in four different buildings, one breezeway connecting them, another one leading to the gymnasium. At one time, the school had added overflow trailers to the mix because of the increasing population in Briar Ridge, but they had sat empty since the school shooting. So many families had left Briar Ridge because of the trauma and the national publicity had kept others from moving to town.

The plans for the new building were a different layout with everything housed in one building. There was only one main entrance, which would be locked during the day for security reasons. She hoped that would soothe parents' concerns and that the new football field and stands would be a draw.

Two teachers' cars sat in the lot along with the custodian's truck. Although the teachers had worked in advance to clean out their classrooms, clearing the entire building of everything that needed to be moved was a major undertaking. The county superintendent of schools had hired a crew to transfer furniture, kitchen equipment, desks and chairs, bulletin boards and other large items. Kate wished they could afford brand-new furnishings for the new building, but the budget wouldn't allow it.

She slipped into her office and spent a couple of hours cleaning out files, discarding papers and other expendable items. Then she packed some paperwork to take home.

For a moment, nostalgia wrapped her in its sentimental folds like a warm blanket. She ran her hand over the scarred wooden surface of her desk. The oak piece had belonged to her mother when she'd taught at Briar Ridge High. It was so special, Kate couldn't bear to part with it.

After her mother died, Kate had moved the desk to her house. The place where her mother had once sat had served as a constant reminder of her strength, patience and positive attitude while Kate studied for her teaching degree and then her Masters.

The same desk and memories would travel with her during the next phase into the new building.

Another wave of nostalgia washed over Kate as she packed the photographs on the wall in her office. There were several of her mother, staff members and teachers, along pictures of Kate when she was a little girl. An eight-by-ten of her and her mother Kate's freshman year at Briar Ridge, all pigtails, braces and pudgy awkwardness, resurrected a bittersweet memory.

One of the mean girls had teased her about her weight. After school, her mother had taken her to the bookstore, and they'd come home with a bag of magazines. Together they'd looked at photos of women in all sizes, shapes, colors and nationalities, Kate's mother pointing out the beauty in each of the women. That day Kate had learned to love her body image and ignore kids who didn't appreciate people's uniqueness.

Unlike Brynn's mother, Kate's had embraced individuality and taught Kate to look beneath the surface. Her mother had also been one of the first in town to advocate for the immigrants who'd moved to Briar Ridge.

She hadn't deserved to die.

Kate sucked in a pain-filled breath. Sometimes, out of the blue, the grief still swept over her in horrific waves.

Leaning forward, hands on her knees, she inhaled deep breaths to ward off her emotions.

Finally regaining her equilibrium, she pressed a kiss to her fingers and touched her mother's face in the photograph. "You told me to make something good happen. I'm trying, Mama. I want you to know that and to be proud."

The sunlight flickering through the window reminded her of the time, and she checked the parking lot. The teachers' cars were gone, but Jimmy's truck was parked in its spot. He'd worked at the school for over twenty-five years and never failed to do whatever she asked with a smile.

Suddenly the building felt cold and empty. The halls, normally filled with students' and teachers' laughter and chatter, echoed with an eerie quiet.

Anxious to leave, Kate spent another hour downloading files onto her laptop. Just as she finished, a noise startled her. Voices? Footsteps? Students or alumni stopping by for a last look before demolition?

She packed the laptop and other files in her computer bag then headed to the door. Her shoes clicked on the tiled floor as she left her carpeted office and walked across the entryway. The faces of past students swam behind her eyes, their voices echoing in her head. Memories of the first day of school, of pep rallies, debating competitions, science fairs and school dances made the building come alive with hope.

The wind rocked the trees and dark clouds cast a gray fog over the parking lot.

The moment she stepped outdoors, she stopped short, a cold chill ripping through her. The gym, attached to the main building via a breezeway, faced the drive. Across the cement wall in front of her, graffitied in large, blood-red paint:

Leave the Past Alone or Die!

"Is BILLY HODGKINS with you?" Riggs asked Woody as Stone pushed the man toward his police car.

"I ain't got nothing to say," Woody snarled. "I want a lawyer."

Riggs rubbed the back of his neck in frustration while Stone's expression never wavered. But his look indicated he would make Woody talk.

"Anyone else staying in the lodge?" Stone asked.

Woody shrugged, his face pasty white.

"Stay here with him." Stone angled his head so Woody couldn't hear him. "And don't touch him, Riggs. The last thing we need is a lawsuit. A jail cell and a few hours without a drink or whatever drug he's on will likely loosen his tongue."

Riggs gave a slight nod.

After Stone secured Woody in the back seat of his squad car, Stone went to see if he could dig up the bullet casings to send to the lab. Riggs leaned closer to the car window and pinned Woody with an intimidating look.

"Did you come back to town for the reunion?" Riggs asked.

Woody cut his eyes to Riggs. "I ain't never left."

Riggs frowned. He hadn't seen Woody around town, but they didn't exactly hang around in the same circles or frequent the same places. Riggs went to work then home and hung out with the other men in his firehouse. Woody probably frequented the bars and places where he could score drugs.

"Were you at the meeting last night?"

Woody's jaw tightened and he looked down at his lap. Scrapes marred his knuckles and his thumbnail was bloody. Either he worked with his hands or he'd messed with Kate's car.

"How'd your hands get beat up?"

"Construction job," Woody mumbled.

Possibly. "How do you feel about the old school being torn down?"

"I don't give a flip," Woody mumbled. "Ain't got nothin' to do with me."

Riggs made a low sound in his throat. Was Woody spouting off what he thought Riggs wanted to hear or was he telling the truth? "What about Kate McKendrick?"

A snarl curled Woody's lips then he whistled. "She's got a nice rack on her."

Riggs balled his hands into fists to keep from slugging the jerk. "I meant do you support her plans for the new school?"

"I told you I don't care one way or the other. I ain't got kids."

Riggs mulled that statement over. Woody didn't appear to be the political, sentimental or family type. His biggest concern was probably where he'd get his next fix.

"This is no joke, Woody. Did you tamper with Kate's car?"

Woody raised two bushy eyebrows. "You serious? Someone tried to kill her?"

"Did you mess with her car?" Riggs said between clenched teeth.

The sound of Stone's footprints echoed across the gravel. His expression looked worried as he approached. Riggs expected a verbal chastising from Stone for questioning Woody while he was gone.

Woody looked up, fake innocence written on his face as Stone joined them. "I want a lawyer."

Before Riggs could speak, Stone climbed in on the driver's side. "A call just came in. We need to go."

Riggs tensed at Stone's tone then slid into the front passenger side. "What's wrong?"

Stone fired up the engine. "Kate called. Someone painted a threatening message on the school wall."

HE HOVERED IN THE SHADOWS of the wooded area by the school and smiled at the look of fear on Kate McKendrick's face as she studied his message.

She should be afraid.

The witch had stirred up old hurts and secrets no one even knew existed.

Ned Hodgkins had been troubled. A loner. A kid who'd been bullied by his classmates and invisible to the people who should have helped him.

Ned had ruined lives seeking revenge against those who'd wronged him.

He understood the need for revenge.

Only he didn't want the limelight or attention.

He wanted the opposite. To go unnoticed. To fade into the woodwork until he could escape this god-awful town.

But Kate was dredging it all up. Opening painful wounds that would never heal, reminding everyone that Ned might not have acted alone. Raising questions as to Ned's motive and if there were secrets that hadn't yet been exposed.

Of course there were.

There was more to the story than anyone suspected.

Secrets he did not want revealed.

Kate moved closer to study the message on the wall, and adrenaline spiked his blood.

The message was intended as a warning.

He raised the match he held in his hand, struck it and watched the flame burst to life. It sizzled and burned, the hiss of the tiny blaze a balm to his tattered soul. He'd always liked fire, ever since he was a little boy and had hidden in the shadows to watch his mother light her cigarette.

The beauty of the flames eating the matchstick excited him the way nothing else ever had.

If Kate didn't leave the past alone, she'd find out what it was like to feel the heat of the flame against her skin. To watch her precious life go up in flames just like the match between his fingers.

Chapter Eight

The sense that someone was watching her made Kate's skin crawl. She gripped her phone as she scanned the area around the school. Was the person who'd graffitied the wall still here?

Was it the same person who'd tampered with her SUV?

Shivering as she reread the threatening message, she backed toward the school. She'd be safer inside. In her office with the door locked.

A noise from the rear of the building startled her. A metal trash can lid blowing in the wind? Footsteps?

Panic clawed at her and she ran for the building. When she reached the front door, she grabbed it to go inside, but it was locked. She frantically rattled the door then knocked on the glass and rang the security buzzer, hoping Jimmy would hear her.

Through the front glass window, she spotted a shadow hovering near the science lab. "Who's there?" she shouted.

The shadow ducked into the lab, the door closing. Suddenly someone grabbed her from behind. She screamed, jerked away then swung around, prepared to fight for her life.

But Jimmy stood there, looking contrite and worried. The poor man barely weighed a hundred and twenty pounds and his faded jeans and shirt hung on his bony frame. His graying hair stood out in tufts, his wire-rimmed glasses sliding down his nose.

"Sorry, Ms. McKendrick, didn't mean to scare you." His dentures clacked in a nervous rhythm. "I was around back, carrying out some trash. Heard you shouting and came to see what all the commotion was about."

Kate's chest rose and fell with her uneven breathing. Jimmy was almost sixty-five, thin and wiry, and should retire. But he'd become a landmark at the school, had even attended high school here himself when he was young.

"I'm sorry," she said. "I...got locked out, and thought you were in the building."

A siren wailed as the sheriff's squad car raced into the school drive. Stone and Riggs climbed from the car and jogged toward her. Both men halted at the sight of the graffiti.

"Pretty bold to do this in daylight." Stone gestured at Jimmy. "Did you see anything?"

"No, sir," Jimmy said. "I've been cleaning out the cafeteria, then was around back taking trash to the dumpster."

Riggs crossed to Kate, his voice gruff. "Are you okay?"

She nodded. "I saw someone going into the lab."

Stone raised his weapon. "Stay here with Kate," he

told Riggs. "I'll search the building." He got a key from Jimmy.

Riggs ushered Kate and Jimmy beneath a live oak near Stone's squad car.

"Hey, Kate!"

Kate stilled then angled her head to see who'd called her name.

Woody Mathis sat rocking himself back and forth in the back of Stone's squad car. His shifty eyes raked over her with a leer.

She hadn't seen him in a while, but his shaggy beard and greasy hair were hard to forget. Over the years, she'd seen him around town at the store or diner. He'd always been jittery, as if up to no good.

"Ignore him." Riggs situated himself between the car and Kate and urged her a few feet back. "He's high as a kite."

"What did he do?" Kate asked.

"We drove to the old lodge outside of town, looking for Billy. We found Woody instead."

"What happened?" Kate asked.

"Idiot pulled a gun and shot at Stone."

Kate stared at him. "Why would he shoot at Stone?"

Riggs shrugged. "Panicked. Probably had drugs, but he must have flushed them when we knocked on the door."

A shudder rippled through Kate. Woody hadn't been vocal about the school one way or the other. But Ned had shot him years ago, and word was that he suffered from PTSD and had turned to drugs.

Did he blame her for his problems?

Riggs kept himself between Kate and Woody just in case the bastard somehow broke free of the handcuffs.

A minute later, the front door to the school opened and Stone appeared, tugging a young man with him.

"Isn't that the mayor's son?" Riggs asked.

Kate nodded. "Yeah, Brynn's younger brother. Don was a late-in-life baby."

"You have trouble with him at school?" Riggs asked.

"Some," she murmured. "I had to call him into the office more than once this past year. Two days ago, I received an anonymous tip that he brought a weapon to school. Our security officer and I pulled him from class and accompanied him to search his locker."

Riggs cleared his throat. "Was there a weapon?"

"Yes, a pocketknife, although Don was furious and said it didn't belong to him." She shivered. "He said I'd be sorry for embarrassing him."

Riggs scratched his head. He'd seen this kid around town, too. He had an attitude, thought he could get away with anything because his daddy was the mayor. He was especially rude to women, as if he had a chip on his shoulder. Twice he'd caught him stealing Minnie Weaver's tips where she waitressed at the Burger Barn.

He'd made the little twerp give it back. But Don had laughed it off and refused to apologize.

"How did the mayor react when he heard about the incident?" Riggs asked.

"He defended Don," Kate admitted with an eye roll. "Said whoever sent in that tip probably put the knife in Don's locker and I had to find the student and expel him or he'd have my job. But I explained that was counterproductive. We set up the anonymous tip system for everyone's safety."

Stone walked toward them, his expression calm, a contrast to Don's sullen face. The punk sported one of those weird haircuts where it was shaved on one side and the other side hung down over one eye. A diamond stud sparkled from one earlobe and his T-shirt bore the name of a heavy metal band whose song lyrics were tinged with violence against women.

Stone gestured to Don. "Found him in the lab like you said, Kate."

"I didn't do anything wrong. I just went in to get my phone," Don snapped. "I left it here the last day of school."

Riggs exchanged a look with Stone then gestured toward the graffiti on the building. "Did you do that, Don?

The kid's eyes twitched as he looked away. "Hell, no, Ms. McKendrick is picking on me."

"Show me your hands," Stone ordered.

Don gave him a surly look but lifted both hands. "See. I'm clean."

Even from where he was standing, Riggs could see the teenager's hands and clothes were paint-free.

"He could have changed clothes and ditched the dirty ones in the trash," Riggs suggested.

Stone gave a grim nod. "Do you know anything about cars?" Stone asked the kid.

Don shrugged "I know how to drive one. See that fire-engine-red Beamer. It's all mine."

Riggs chewed the inside of his cheek. Typical attitude for a spoiled, entitled kid. And why had he parked his car on the corner instead of the parking lot up front?

"In fact, I need to check in with my father," Don said with a cocky smile. "He's taking me golfing for acing my finals."

Riggs wouldn't be surprised if the boy had cheated.

Stone cleared his throat. "You threatened Ms. McKendrick at school because she searched your locker, didn't you?"

Don shot Kate a nasty look. "I was innocent then and I'm innocent now." Defiance radiated from every pore in the kid's body. "Now, can I go? Or should I call my father and ask him to send his lawyer?"

Stone's eyes darkened. "You can go but stay away from the school and from Ms. McKendrick."

The kid mouthed something Riggs couldn't quite understand, although it sounded foul, then sauntered to the street to his Beamer and slid in. A second later, he peeled away.

"He could have washed up in the lab," Riggs pointed out.

Stone gave a little nod. "I'll have the crime team search there, along with the trash cans and dumpster out back."

"Kate, do you think Don would hurt you?" Riggs asked.

Kate sighed. "I really don't know. He despises me, although I'm not sure why. Maybe he overheard his mother talking about me. Mrs. Gaines forbid Brynn from hanging out with me after the shooting."

Riggs rubbed his forehead. Why wouldn't Mrs. Gaines want Kate to see Brynn?

Stone secured his gun in his holster. "If Don bothers you, call me."

The wind picked up, swirling Kate's hair around her face. She absentmindedly tucked a strand of hair behind her ear. "I will."

"Meanwhile, I'll get a crime team out here to process the building. Maybe we can lift some prints from the graffiti wall. I'll also have them search for paint cans and a ladder." Stone hesitated. "Make a list of any and all students you had trouble with this year. If you expelled someone or put them on probation, rank them at the top of the list. If they're related to one of the victims from our class, note that, as well."

Riggs shifted. If a family member of one of the victims had threatened Kate, that meant everyone in town, including the former students returning for the reunion, was suspect.

KATE RUBBED AT her temple where a headache pulsed. She just wanted to go home and forget about today. But she couldn't escape the terrible sensation that someone hated her enough to want her dead.

Before she and Riggs reached her car, a dark green Lexus rolled into the drive. Kate rubbed her fingers together. Good grief. The car belonged to Gretta.

How had she heard about this incident so quickly?

Gretta squealed to a stop and hopped from her car wearing a hot-pink suit with matching acrylic nails. Her ash-blond hair was swept up in a fancy chignon, emeralds glittering from both ears. She spied the graffiti and snapped a few pictures then made a beeline for them.

Stone stepped in front of the squad car to block her from photographing Woody, who was rocking himself back and forth in the back seat. He must be coming down from his high and needed a fix.

Gretta quickly assessed the scene, addressing Kate. "What happened?"

"Someone vandalized the wall," Stone cut in, his voice dry. "How did you find out?"

"I have my sources." Gretta shrugged nonchalantly.

Kate bit back a comment. Gretta was a calculating, coldhearted woman who'd sacrifice her own mother for a byline. She'd never revealed how she'd gotten the scoop on students and exposed their secrets. She also hadn't cared who she'd hurt.

Judging from recent incriminating pieces she'd written about a Ponzi scheme involving her own brother, she obviously hadn't changed.

Gretta gestured at the police car. "Have you already made an arrest?"

Stone waved his hand dismissively. "No. I'm bringing Woody in on a separate matter. And I'd better not see a reference to him in the paper. Now, get out of here, Gretta. I have a crime to investigate."

"I have a right to be here, Sheriff. The people in town need to be alerted if there's a criminal loose," Gretta said, then asked Kate, "Did you see who did this?"

Kate shook her head. She didn't intend to feed Gretta any information. No telling how the woman might construe what she said. "No."

"What about your car catching on fire?"

Kate tensed. Was Gretta simply being her nosy self or did she know more than she wanted to say?

She inched closer and touched Kate's arm in a sympathetic gesture. "That must have been terrifying."

Riggs spoke before Kate could. "What do you know about the fire, Gretta?"

Gretta released a dramatic sigh. "Just that it was suspicious. If someone is trying to hurt the school principal or anyone else in town, the residents need to be warned. And maybe the reunion activities should be cancelled."

Kate frowned. What if that was the purpose of the threats?

"As I said, I have no comment at this time," Stone said sharply. "And if you interfere, I'll arrest you."

Gretta released a long-winded sigh. "Seriously, Stone. Let's be honest here. I witnessed the volatile reactions at the town meeting," Gretta said. "And I know someone tampered with Kate's SUV. Do you have any idea who did it?"

Kate's temper surfaced. "No, I don't. Do *you*?"

Gretta's catlike eyes flashed with a warning. "No, but if you don't share information, I'll find out on my own."

Jaw clenched, Stone straightened to his full six-two. "Don't interfere with my investigation, Gretta."

"I'm just doing my job, Sheriff. Like it or not, Kate's campaign to tear down this building and replace it opened old wounds. If there's someone dangerous lurking around, people should be aware so they can protect themselves. Just look what happened with Ned Hodgkins." Gretta aimed an accusatory look toward Kate. "Maybe if we'd been warned he was so depressed that he was dangerous, someone could have stopped him and lives wouldn't have been lost."

Kate's lungs squeezed for air. Gretta was right.

If she'd accepted Ned's invitation to the dance, she might have picked up on his anxiety and depression.

Then *she* could have saved lives. Including her mother's.

Chapter Nine

Riggs clenched his hands by his sides. He'd never, ever, been rough with a woman. But Gretta's cutthroat techniques tempted him to physically shake her.

She'd always been trouble. He hadn't liked her in high school, and he sure as hell didn't like the way she was pushing Kate now. "Come on, Kate. Let's get out of here."

Kate crossed her arms over her chest and gave Gretta a chilly look. "I have nothing to say to you now, Gretta, and I never will."

A spark of admiration for Kate stirred inside Riggs. Kate might have backed away from trouble as a teenager, but she'd stood her ground with Gretta the same way she had with protestors at the meeting.

"Thank you, Stone," Kate said. "I'll get that list to you as soon as possible."

"I'm going to talk to Jimmy," Stone said. "Maybe he saw more than he thought he did."

Kate murmured okay then started to walk away and dismiss Riggs. But Riggs didn't intend to allow her to go home alone so he rushed to catch up with her. What if Billy was waiting?

And if Billy hadn't painted the graffiti, the culprit might have hung around to see Kate's reaction. He also might be stalking Kate.

Gretta was watching them as if she sensed they were keeping something from her, so he lowered his voice to a conspiratorial whisper.

"I rode with Stone," he said. "Do you mind dropping me by the station to pick up my truck? Then I'll follow you home and make sure no one is lurking around."

Her gaze darted back to Gretta as if she expected the woman to pounce again. But Gretta had finally turned her attention back to work and was snapping pictures of the graffiti.

"I suppose I could do that. I owe you one."

Riggs brushed her arm with his fingers. "You don't owe me anything, Kate."

Her bright blue eyes met his, worry and fear mingling with other emotions he couldn't quite define.

She obviously didn't want to spend any more time with him than she had to.

He squashed the hurt that realization triggered. It didn't matter what she thought of him. All that mattered was keeping her safe.

"All right, let's go." She checked her watch. "I'm supposed to meet the security company soon."

Riggs followed her to her rental SUV. Maybe on the drive to the police station, Kate would tell him more about Don Gaines and the reason he harbored such animosity toward her.

KATE FELT GRETTA'S scrutinizing gaze as she'd walked to her car. She shouldn't let the woman bother her, but old scars ran deep.

Darn it, she was trying to move on with her life and make positive changes. Why couldn't she shake the hurt that woman had caused with her juvenile gossip rag?

Quickly starting the engine, she pulled onto the road leading back to town.

She didn't trust Gretta. The woman was a user and didn't care who she walked all over to get her story. More than once she'd lied about classmates to stir up a frenzy and create drama and conflict.

Sure, she'd retracted the story later on, claiming her source had been misinformed. But the damage had been done.

Kate didn't believe the source was the problem, either. Gretta was a thrill-seeking, attention-hungry, manipulative liar. Embellishment was her trademark.

"I admire the way you stood up to Gretta," Riggs murmured.

His approval sent a warm feeling through her. Why, she didn't know. She and Riggs were simply acquaintances.

Although she was grateful for his support over the new school. With his popularity in town, he might sway others to come around.

They reached the police station, and she swerved into the parking spot beside Riggs's pickup then angled her head to study him.

"Why are you being so nice to me?" Kate asked.

Riggs shrugged. "Maybe I'm a nice guy."

Kate laughed softly.

"That's funny?" Hurt tinged his eyes.

"No, it's just that I can't figure you out. Here you are babysitting me on your day off when you could be out having fun with one of your women."

Riggs arched a brow. "One of my *women*?"

A blush crept up Kate's neck. "You know what I mean."

A muscle ticked in his jaw. "You think all I do is screw around, don't you?"

She bit her lip, sensing she'd offended him. "It's not a criticism. We're not even friends, so what you do on your own time is none of my business."

"Right." Pulse hammering, he reached for the door handle. "Maybe I did screw around in school, and afterward for a while." His voice thickened. "But people change, Kate. *I've* changed."

Riggs Benford had changed? He wasn't a womanizer now?

Seriously?

"I didn't mean to offend you, Riggs."

He squared his shoulders. "I didn't realize you were so judgmental, Kate."

For a moment, Kate simply stared at him. She felt as if she'd been reprimanded.

But he was right. For all her talk about being positive and moving forward, she still saw Riggs as the teenage flirt he'd been in high school.

Yet on some level she knew he had changed. He risked his life to save others. She'd also heard he visited the children's hospital in his uniform to cheer up sick children.

"I really am sorry," Kate said. "I've lived alone a long time, Riggs. I'm not used to answering to anyone."

His eyes turned smoldering. Intense. She hadn't felt this kind of sexual awareness in…she couldn't even remember.

She didn't want to feel it for Riggs.

Still, for a brief second, she couldn't drag her gaze from his. Her body tingled as if his fingers were raking over her just as his eyes were. Heat stirred deep inside her, dormant needs and fantasies simmering beneath the surface.

It had been forever since someone had held her. Kissed her. Loved her.

She missed being touched. Missed the intimacy.

Most of all, she missed having someone to share her thoughts and dreams with.

The one guy she'd dated in college certainly hadn't wanted to talk. And he definitely hadn't wanted a future with her.

She jerked her mind back to reality.

Sexy or not, Riggs had abandoned his child. He might volunteer at the children's hospital, but his own son lived in Briar Ridge and he'd never even acknowledged him.

"We may not have been friends in the past," Riggs said, "but we could start now."

Kate's breath quickened.

Riggs stared at her for a long tense minute, as if

hoping she'd say something, but she clamped her teeth over her bottom lip.

A second later, something akin to disappointment flashed in his eyes before he climbed out, strode to his truck and got in.

Tension coiled inside her as she pulled from the parking lot and headed for her house.

But Riggs's words taunted her as she drove.

Yes, they could be friends. But it terrified her that she might want more…

RIGGS FOUGHT ANGER at Kate's reaction as he followed her. Not that he blamed her for her opinion. At one time, he'd welcomed the reputation as a love-'em-and-leave-'em kind of guy. No strings attached, no commitments, no one to tie him down. That had been his motto.

But he had changed, dammit. Had started to want more.

It bothered him that Kate couldn't see deeper than the surface.

That she must believe the rumors about him and Cassidy and that baby. A baby that was now a fifteen-year-old teenager. One who attended Briar Ridge High.

He had no idea what Cassidy had told her son about his father. He sure as hell didn't think she'd told the boy he was his daddy.

But who really knew what Cassidy would do? She was brash, unpredictable and needy.

On Saturday night, she frequented bars dressed in low-cut tops and miniskirts, hanging on any guy who'd buy her a drink. Sure, she had the same right as a man to put herself out there. But she couldn't handle her liquor and didn't discriminate about who she took home to bed. Rumors surfaced that she traded sex for drugs on occasion. Made him wonder what kind of mother she was to her son.

Roy. That's the name Cassidy had given the boy. He was thin, gangly, and wore dark square-framed glasses. Riggs had seen him at the arcade, totally enthralled in video games. And he was always alone, as if he had no friends.

Not your problem.

Neither was Kate.

But here he was following her to her house like a lovesick puppy, declaring himself her protector when she clearly did not want his protection.

But, dammit, he cared what happened to her.

It's just because she's in danger. You could never be what Kate wants. A husband... Father to her kids... You're too much like your old man.

No...hell no, he wasn't. He'd worked hard not to be like him at all.

His father had been mean and cold and talked with his fists. The best thing his mother ever did was leave him. Riggs just didn't understand why she hadn't taken him with her.

Better to stay single. Unattached. Guard his heart.

Kate parked in her drive, climbed out and hurried up her porch steps. He parked beside her, leaving room for the driver from the security company, and surveying her property as he walked up to her porch.

More dark clouds rumbled above, casting an ominous gray over the mountains and adding a chill to the air. One of Kate's shutters had come loose and flapped against the pale blue siding.

She unlocked the front door and hurried inside just as he stepped onto the welcome mat.

Although he didn't feel welcome at Kate's, and that bugged the hell out of him.

She paused at the door, the dim light painting lines around her heart-shaped face. "Thanks for making sure I got home okay," she said softly. The shutter flapped again, and she startled.

He jammed his hands into his pockets, determined to remain cool. "Sure. If you have a hammer and some nails, I'll repair that shutter."

She looked as if she was going to argue, but the shutter banged again. "Thanks, but I can fix it myself."

God, she was stubborn. "It's no problem, Kate. I'll repair it while the security company installs your system."

She hesitated, and his gut tightened. "Are you afraid of me?" he asked gruffly.

Her eyes widened and she clamped her teeth over her bottom lip.

"You are, aren't you?" His chest throbbed at the thought.

"No," she said quickly. "I'm just nervous about the threats." She shrugged. "Besides, I'm not used to relying on a man to take care of things for me."

He raised a brow at that. "Then you've been hanging out with the wrong men. You deserve someone who'll treat you right, Kate."

Suddenly he wanted to be that man.

Her eyes searched his again, as if she was trying to figure him out. Indecision warred in his mind, but he decided he had to win her trust.

That meant being honest and sharing something he'd never told a damn soul.

"Can I come in a minute?" he asked gruffly. "We should talk."

Wariness darkened her eyes but she stepped aside and gestured for him to enter. "I guess that would be all right."

He entered the foyer, rubbing a hand down his neck. "I know you don't trust me, but I swear I would never hurt you, Kate."

"Then tell me why you're really doing this."

Man, she was direct. He wanted to say because he liked her. But that was putting himself on the line. And judging from her reaction, she didn't want to hear it.

"Because I owe your mother," he admitted.

Her brow furrowed and she folded her arms across her chest. "What do you mean?"

He ground his teeth, struggling for the courage to admit the truth. "Yeah. She was good to me."

"She was good to all her students," Kate said softly.

"I know." He shifted, uncomfortable, but he'd started this and he was going to damn well finish. "I was having trouble in school," he said. "I thought I was going to lose my position on the soccer team, lose my chance at a scholarship. All the rumors about me didn't help."

Cleary, he'd said the wrong thing, because suspicions flared in her eyes.

Damn, she thought he was referring to Cassidy.

KATE ORDERED HERSELF to keep an open mind. Maybe there were two sides to the story about him and Cassidy. Perhaps he'd tried to be a father to the boy and Cassidy had rejected him for some reason.

Although she couldn't imagine anyone rejecting Riggs.

"It's not what you think," he said quickly. "I don't mean trouble as in the law or with a *girl*," he said pointedly. "I had trouble reading. I struggled through classes and got poor grades. But your mother picked up on the source of the problem."

Surprise made her stomach tighten. "You're dyslexic?"

He nodded then cast his head down slightly. "Kids laughed and teased me when I was little. I failed classes. They called me names—stupid, idiot." He blew out a breath. "I thought I was stupid. So did my father, and he never missed a chance to tell me."

Compassion filled Kate as she pictured Riggs as a little boy being laughed at. And angry at his father who should have supported him.

Although she remembered hearing that Riggs's father had been abusive.

The truth dawned on her. Riggs's cocky, tough-guy attitude had been a cover-up so no one would see his pain.

"Oh, Riggs," Kate said gently. "Dyslexia doesn't mean you aren't intelligent. It's a learning disability."

Anguish twisted his face. "I know that. At least, I do now. Your mother tutored me in private and taught me techniques to read so I could pass my classes and stay on the soccer team."

Tenderness for Riggs welled inside Kate. Just like everyone else, she'd only seen the surface side of Riggs. And she'd made judgments based on his appearance and his past when he was just a kid.

Her mother would not be pleased with how she'd been treating him.

He was a man now. They were both different people.

"I'm glad my mother recognized the problem and that she helped you. She'd be proud of the man you've become."

A relieved look settled in Riggs's eyes, making him look so vulnerable that Kate ached to comfort him.

Then a look of masculine desire filled his eyes and her heart fluttered.

"She'd be proud of you, too, Kate," he said softly. "Proud of what you're trying to do for the town."

Forgetting all her reservations, Kate took a step closer, her heart hammering.

She lifted her hand and stroked his jaw, heat stirring inside her as her fingers brushed his coarse beard stubble.

God help her. Riggs was all masculinity and sexual prowess.

She wanted to kiss him so badly, her mouth watered.

Desire flared in his eyes as if he felt the pull between them. But just as he angled his head and moved toward her, the doorbell rang.

Kate started and Riggs growled a curse.

The security company had arrived and saved her from making a fool out of herself.

HE STRUCK THE match and watched the flame flicker to life. Fire had always fascinated him.

The sudden burst of orange and red and yellow. The heat rolling off the fire. The way the flames caught and spread so quickly, feeding on oxygen and eating up everything in its path.

It was a thing of pure beauty.

It could also be deadly.

His pulse jumped as the flame burned bright and tall, leaping and dancing against the darkening sky, consuming the matchstick until it disintegrated in his fingers. Heat scalded the tip of his thumb and he tossed the last of the match to the ground, then sucked his thumb into his mouth to ward off the sting.

The flame started to die in the brush, but a gust of wind resurrected it and embers burst to life in the thick straw and broken tree limbs. He glanced around the wooded area.

It was deserted. No one knew he was there.

No one would.

He should stomp out the fire. But he was mesmerized by the way it started to grow, slowly jumping from one patch of brush to another. Broken pieces of tree limbs and pine straw crackled and popped, the flames rippling through the forest, creating a path of destruction in its wake.

Heat seared his skin as the fire intensified. Flames shot upward and smoke thickened the air, creating a gray fog. Memories surfaced. The first time he'd played with matches.

He'd seen his mama take a man into her bedroom. Heard them grunting and groaning. Saw the chubby man walk out naked, sweat pouring off him as he grabbed another beer and carried it into the bedroom.

He'd wanted to burn down the house that night.

Kill that bastard.

When the man finally staggered out to his truck and roared away, he'd been relieved. Then he'd seen his mama passed out with her bottle.

He'd covered her naked body with a blanket and then snatched her Camels and matches and slipped outside. First, the old metal trash can. He lit the cigarette, inhaled and coughed his head off. He'd dropped it in the can and it had caught the trash. Paper and plastic melted and sizzled. The flames had grown bolder, shooting up from the can.

While his mother had slept off her drunk, he'd gone inside, broken one of the kitchen chairs, carried it to the backyard, and fed it to the flames.

He'd fallen asleep by the firelight, smiling as he'd imagined it spreading to the house and taking his mother with it.

The next day, she'd never even noticed. From then on, fire had become his obsession.

Now he inhaled the pungent odor of burning wood and excitement zinged through him as the flames raced along the forest floor. A patch of fire slithered up a thin pine and lit the sky as the needles caught.

Houses lay nearby, just beyond the hill.

Kate McKendrick's house.

Another smile tugged at his mouth.

Seconds later, a siren wailed in the distance. Someone had seen the smoke and called it in.

Heart hammering, he turned and ran back through the woods to where he could hide and watch the chaos.

Chapter Ten

Riggs gritted his teeth as Kate rushed to answer the door. Dammit, if he hadn't misread the situation, Kate had been about to kiss him.

He could still feel her gentle fingers on his cheek. He wanted to feel them in other places, his bare chest, his back, his hips…

He wanted to return the favor and erase the fear in her eyes with pleasure.

"Yes, please come on in," Kate was saying to the consultant from the security company.

She avoided eye contact with Riggs as she led the uniformed man inside.

Fool. Kate had simply felt sorry for him because of his confession. Nothing more.

Jaw tight, he cleared his throat. "Excuse me, Kate. Where's your toolbox?"

"The garage." Unease flickered in her eyes. Regret?

Tamping down his lust, he strode to the door leading to her garage, leaving her alone to deal with the security consultant.

Her garage was neat and organized. Gardening tools

in one section, a bike in the corner, camping gear in another. A wall of shelves housed her toolbox and other supplies.

Living alone had obviously taught Kate to be independent. He wondered why she'd never married and had a family. Kate seemed like she'd have a passel of kids. Did she have a boyfriend hiding in the woodwork?

If so, where was he now?

Disturbed at the possibility, Riggs carried the toolbox and ladder outside and tackled the repair job.

Just as he finished, the scent of smoke assaulted him.

Senses jumping to alert, he climbed higher on the ladder and surveyed Kate's property. Nothing on fire in the yard.

But… God. In the woods behind her house, smoke curled into the sky and flames licked at the trees and brush, burning through the forest as the wind picked up and fueled its path.

At the rate it was going and with the direction of the wind, it would take no time for it to reach the houses in Kate's neighborhood.

Sweat beaded his skin and he snagged his phone and called the fire station. His captain answered on the third ring.

"A fire at Kate McKendrick's house," Riggs said.

"Someone else called it in already. We're on our way," his boss said.

Riggs didn't like how close it was to Kate's. "I'll meet you there."

He ended the call, jumped from the ladder and

rushed to tell Kate where he was going. The fire could have started accidentally.

But considering what had happened with Kate's car and the threats she'd received, it could have been meant for Kate.

THE SECURITY CONSULTANT was installing the alarm pad in her bedroom when Kate glanced through the sliders in her den and noticed smoke. The gray cloud swirled above the treetops, weaving through the spiny needles of the pines and spiraling into the dark sky.

A second later, Riggs rushed in, his face a mask of professionalism although his eyes suggested he wasn't as calm as he appeared.

"The woods—"

"I just saw the smoke," Kate said.

"I'm going to meet my unit there. With the wind gusts, we need to contain it fast."

Kate sucked in a breath. Riggs's job meant running into burning buildings on a daily basis, but the thought of him battling that blaze in the woods sent a streak of terror through her.

"Will you be okay here?" Riggs asked.

Kate couldn't believe he was worried about her when he was the one who faced danger every day. "I'll be fine, Riggs. But you need to be careful."

"Always am, Kate. I know what I'm doing."

Of course he did. "That doesn't mean you can't get hurt."

A smile deepened the grooves at the corner of his mouth, replacing that brooding look and showcasing that sexy dimple. He reached out and stroked her arm. "Don't worry. I'll be back."

She said a silent prayer that he would be as he rushed out the door. Nerves on edge, she walked to the sliding-glass doors, opened them and stepped outside. The scent of smoke, burning wood and charred grass wafted toward her, clogging the fresh mountain air.

The wind picked up again, blowing through the trees and pushing the fire her way. She heard the distant sound of a siren wailing, and imagined Riggs's team descending on the blaze, working to protect her and others in the fire's wake.

Riggs had been such a tease in high school, always cracking jokes and flirting. She'd never imagined he had a serious side. Although, after the shooting, he'd been in pain and had to do physical therapy.

You also didn't know he was dyslexic. You just assumed his good looks and cocky attitude meant he was full of himself. But maybe it was an act to cover his insecurities.

No... Riggs didn't have an insecure bone in his body.

Except he had seemed vulnerable when he'd confided about being teased. And one lesson they all should have learned from Ned was not to assume anything, to dig deeper and uncover what was really going on in a person's head, not to judge someone on the sake of appearances.

"Ma'am, I'm finished."

The consultant's voice broke the silence and Kate closed the sliding-glass door.

"Let me show you the ins and outs," he said, eyes

darting to the clouds of smoke above the tree line. "I also installed the doorbell camera as you requested."

Relief spilled through Kate. At least she would know if someone tried to break in. "Thank you."

He spent the next half hour explaining the ins and outs of the system and then asked for a security code word.

Kate glanced at the sliding doors again, her heart pounding at the sight of the flames ripping through the woods.

In spite of the fear clawing at her, she chose the word *Hopeful*.

There's always hope for good, her mother used to say.

Kate intended to cling to her mother's mantra as long as she lived.

RIGGS SUITED UP as soon as he made it to the side of the road where the fire trucks were parked. Acres of wooded property and farmland dotted the mountainous area. Tall pines, oaks and evergreens climbed upward, the first signs of summer evident in the wildflowers pushing through the green. White blossoms from the dogwoods looked like snow as they fluttered to the ground, and birds soared above, returning from their winter trek to the south.

His fellow firefighters were already busy rolling hoses as far as they could reach. A special team had been called to fly above and unleash water on the blaze.

Containment was key for the safety of the residents who lived nearby.

They weren't ordering evacuations yet, but if the

blaze spread another mile and the winds gained speed, the houses in Kate's neighborhood would be in serious danger.

So would Kate.

"Do we know cause yet?" he asked Brian who'd arrived first on the scene with Riggs's coworkers.

"Not yet," Brian said. "So far, it's spread about a quarter of a mile through the woods. The volunteer team from the neighboring county is on its way. We need all the manpower we can get."

"Be on the lookout for signs of arson," Riggs said as he strapped on his helmet.

Brian frowned. "You think it was intentional?"

Riggs shrugged. He didn't want to elaborate yet, but they had to consider all scenarios. "It's possible."

Although, if the fire had nothing to do with Kate, and it was arson, it could have been set to cover up a crime. It was one of the most common causes of arson.

With bitterness pervading the town and former classmates returning, who knew what old vendettas might come into play. Stones had been cast after the shooting, friendships shattered, blame tossed around like live grenades.

Riggs and the men dove into their work, attacking the blaze and tracking it through the woods, creating barriers and soaking the grounds in the fire's path. Others worked to dump water on the flames, a second plane joining the first to cover more territory.

He lost track of time as they worked, simply went into autopilot. Sweat beaded his skin and trickled down his neck, the thickening smoke making it imperative to breathe through his mask. Tree limbs cracked and popped, the heat intensifying. He and his coworkers dodged the falling fiery debris as it snapped off with the weight of the water assaulting the flames.

His boots smashed dying embers, twigs and brush soaked by the water, the scent of fire all around him. Riggs worked for a good two hours with his crew before the blaze began to die down and the air became clear enough to see in front of him.

"The fire is contained," the chief said over Riggs's mic. "I repeat, it's contained, but we'll monitor it overnight."

Riggs and Brian traded relieved looks. "Do you have any idea the point of origin?" Riggs asked.

"We have a general idea," Brian murmured.

The chief spoke again. "Sheriff Stone is at the scene. He's calling in deputies to cordon off and guard the area until we can search for forensics and an accelerant."

So far, Riggs hadn't detected the scent of gasoline. But he could be a half mile from point of origin.

"Thanks for the assist," Brian said as they stowed their gear on the truck. "Hope we didn't tear you away from a hot date."

Riggs made a low sound in his throat. He wished to hell he had been on a date with Kate. But she'd probably turn him down if he asked.

Then another disturbing thought struck him. Perhaps the arsonist set the fire to lure Riggs and the police away from her.

Dammit.

He had to get back and check on Kate.

KATE SHOULD HAVE felt safe with the new security system intact, but each time she looked outside at the smoke-filled sky, her heart pounded with fear for Riggs.

Needing to stay busy, she spent over an hour on the paperwork she'd brought home. Stone's request for the list of students she'd had trouble with nagged at her, so she'd powered up her laptop and run a search for students that had required disciplinary action.

First, a group of kids caught smoking pot in the parking lot: a senior girl and two sophomore boys. She'd suspended them for three days, conferenced with their parents, and allowed them to return to school on probation. The teens had been upset, but they were loners and pacifists, free thinkers and nonconformists that'd never exhibited signs of violence.

Next, she looked at minor infractions—skipping school, cheating, pranks, smoking—but again, none of those students would retaliate with such a degree of violence.

She drummed her fingernails on her lap then examined three students caught fighting in the cafeteria. The first, Darius Holbrook, had moved to Tennessee the second semester. His parents claimed kids were bullying their son and he'd fought back in self-defense. Kate had checked out the story and found it was true, so she'd taken action against the bullies and required them to attend counseling.

She hadn't received reports of their fighting since.

The graffiti incident taunted her. Don Gaines had been at the school, where, she also knew, he'd excelled in art class. She searched for reports of him causing trouble or being involved in any incident of violence. He had been caught smoking in the bathrooms and outside the school. The first time, cigarettes, the second time, weed.

She didn't want to believe Brynn's brother would try to scare her by graffitiing that threat on the side of the school.

Still, Don disliked her. Maybe he knew she was the reason Ned had gone ballistic and shot his sister. The entire family had suffered and been traumatized because of Brynn's paralysis. Mrs. Gaines had always doted on Brynn. No doubt the shooting and Brynn's injury had made that worse. She'd always had high expectations for Brynn. How had she handled the disappointment that Brynn wouldn't walk again? Had she given her attention to Don instead and smothered him?

Or had all her attention been focused on Brynn?

Could Don want revenge for the devastation his family suffered because of the shooting?

FLASHLIGHT IN HAND, Riggs searched the ground as he walked back up the hill toward his truck. The brittle brush, ashes and dying embers made it difficult to see, especially in the dark, but at first light when the area cooled, a full crime scene team would be out hunting for forensics.

A piece of clothing, hair, footprints, accelerant— anything they could use to pinpoint whether the fire was accidental or arson.

His boots dug into the earth, now wet from their efforts to douse the flames, and a patch of weeds shifted.

He shone the light onto the patch and spotted something small stuck in the burned leaves, almost hidden by a river rock.

Pulse jumping, he knelt and gently raked the weeds aside.

A matchbook.

Pulling gloves from his pocket, surprised it hadn't completely been destroyed in the fire, he carefully lifted and examined it. The matchbook was empty, the edges charred. He wiped away soot and recognized the logo on the front—Smokehouse Barbecue.

Could it have belonged to the person who'd set this fire? Anger hardened his jaw and Riggs secured it in a bag to give to Stone to send to the lab.

The matchbook could mean nothing. People hiked in the woods all the time.

But it could be a lead. If a match from this book had been used to set the fire, and the lab could pull fingerprints, it might lead to the responsible party.

Accidental or not, this fire could have taken lives.

And if it was intentional, and they were dealing with an arsonist, he needed to be stopped before he struck again.

Complete the survey below and return it today to receive up to **4 FREE BOOKS** and **FREE GIFTS** guaranteed!

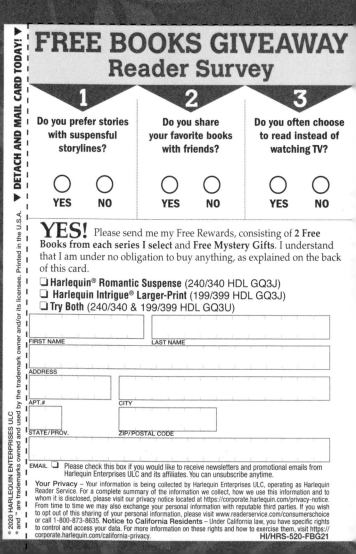

▼ DETACH AND MAIL CARD TODAY! ▼

FREE BOOKS GIVEAWAY
Reader Survey

1
Do you prefer stories with suspensful storylines?

◯ YES ◯ NO

2
Do you share your favorite books with friends?

◯ YES ◯ NO

3
Do you often choose to read instead of watching TV?

◯ YES ◯ NO

YES! Please send me my Free Rewards, consisting of **2 Free Books from each series I select** and **Free Mystery Gifts**. I understand that I am under no obligation to buy anything, as explained on the back of this card.

❑ Harlequin® Romantic Suspense (240/340 HDL GQ3J)
❑ Harlequin Intrigue® Larger-Print (199/399 HDL GQ3J)
❑ Try Both (240/340 & 199/399 HDL GQ3U)

FIRST NAME | LAST NAME

ADDRESS

APT.# | CITY

STATE/PROV. | ZIP/POSTAL CODE

EMAIL ❑ Please check this box if you would like to receive newsletters and promotional emails from Harlequin Enterprises ULC and its affiliates. You can unsubscribe anytime.

Your Privacy – Your information is being collected by Harlequin Enterprises ULC, operating as Harlequin Reader Service. For a complete summary of the information we collect, how we use this information and to whom it is disclosed, please visit our privacy notice located at https://corporate.harlequin.com/privacy-notice. From time to time we may also exchange your personal information with reputable third parties. If you wish to opt out of this sharing of your personal information, please visit www.readerservice.com/consumerschoice or call 1-800-873-8635. **Notice to California Residents** – Under California law, you have specific rights to control and access your data. For more information on these rights and how to exercise them, visit https://corporate.harlequin.com/california-privacy.

HI/HRS-520-FBG21

© 2020 HARLEQUIN ENTERPRISES ULC
® and ™ are trademarks owned and used by the trademark owner and/or its licensee. Printed in the U.S.A.

Chapter Eleven

Riggs backtracked to give Stone the matchbook and found Macy Stark standing beside him, looking concerned as she glanced across the charred woods.

"Good work," Stone said. "I'll have the lab run it for forensics."

"What happened with Woody?" Riggs asked.

Stone shrugged. "Guy's a mess and needs rehab. No confession, and no proof that he's done anything. I'm going to have to cut him loose."

Riggs indicated the matchbook. "Is he a smoker?"

Stone's eyebrows drew together in a frown. "Yeah, matter of fact, he begged for a cigarette. But he's still in a holding cell, so he couldn't have started this fire."

Stone nodded. "But Billy could have."

"He's on my list to question," Stone said before being called away by one of his deputies.

Macy cleared her throat. "Do you think someone intentionally set the fire?"

Riggs shrugged. "Considering the threats to Kate and the point of origin being in close proximity to her house, we have to consider that possibility."

Macy rubbed at her arm, drawing attention to the sling. She was taller than Kate, her long black hair wavy, her green eyes as sharp as a cat's. She'd been physically fit in high school, competitive, a good athlete and the fastest sprinter on the track team.

Macy had always seemed intense, almost aloof at times, unlike sweet Kate, or Brynn with her golden-blond hair, fashion sense, and beauty pageant titles who thrived on being in the social limelight.

The three were so different that he'd thought their friendship odd, but something had drawn them together.

So what had torn them apart?

Macy's voice resonated with concern. "How's Kate?"

"Shaken," Riggs answered. "Haven't you seen her since you got to town?"

Macy glanced back at the woods, a distant look in her eyes. "I saw her after her car caught fire, but we haven't talked."

Curiosity got the better of him. "What's going on?"

Her mouth tightened. "Nothing. I just have a lot to do. I came to clear out my mother's house and get it ready to sell."

Riggs dug his hands in his pockets. He'd heard rumors about Macy's mother having psychological problems, that she'd been institutionalized, and didn't know what to say. "Does that mean you'll be in town for a while?"

"Just until after the dedication ceremony and I put the house on the market."

"Stone said he asked you to look over the files about the shooting."

Macy's expression darkened. "He did. Everyone wants to know if Ned acted alone."

Stone walked back toward them, clipping his phone on his belt. "Crime team is on its way here. I'll meet the deputies and hang around until they rope off the area."

"Did they find forensics on the graffiti wall or anything from the trash cans?" Riggs asked.

"Lifted some partials off the wall. We'll compare them to Don's. No discarded paint-stained clothes, though."

"Someone from the firehouse will stay overnight to make sure the blaze doesn't reignite," Riggs said.

The sound of a car engine rumbled and Gretta's Lexus careened onto the side of the road, pulling to a stop behind the sheriff's car.

"I'll check on Kate," Riggs said. "Keep me posted on the lab results."

Stone muttered he would, and Riggs hiked back toward his truck, determined to avoid the pushy reporter who'd fueled the rumors about his relationship with Cassidy. One afternoon she'd hid behind the bleachers and snapped a picture of him and Cassidy arguing. He'd been trying to convince Cassidy to tell him if he was her baby's father, but she'd refused to talk. That photograph had painted him as a hothead and made Cassidy look like a victim.

If Gretta learned about the letter of blame Kate had received or that Kate felt guilty for Ned's actions, she would plaster it all over the paper and make things worse for Kate.

He ordered himself not to care, but he didn't want

to see Kate hurt, especially by someone as conniving and unethical as Gretta.

He went still as a disturbing thought struck him. What if Gretta had sent the letter to Kate? Would she stir up trouble in town to enhance her story?

KATE FINISHED THE list for Stone, although she was hesitant to toss accusations at innocent students.

Then again, she couldn't ignore the facts or students' behavior—that was part of her job. If someone had noticed how deeply troubled Ned had been, he could have been helped and lives wouldn't have been lost.

She'd made it a policy to instill programs to prevent bullying, to open doors for lonely students to find friends, and had always examined the larger picture when a student acted out. Digging into their family lives often revealed the reasons for their misbehavior. Instead of harsh punishment, students needed counseling and love, to be taught coping skills to deal with their problems.

She pulled the yearbook from her senior year and thumbed through it. A photograph of Macy crossing the finish line first when Briar Ridge went to State brought a pang to her heart.

After the win, Macy had celebrated with the track team and been excited over the prospect of running in college. When she'd gone home that night, her mother had locked Macy out of the house again. She'd been enraged that Macy had been at a school meet instead of at home taking care of her.

Macy had run to Kate's in tears, and Kate had stayed

up with her half the night, consoling her. Her mother had made them brownies and hot chocolate, and assured Macy that she should be proud of herself.

Kate's heart swelled with love and pride for her mother as another memory surfaced. One much earlier, when she'd first learned Macy's mother had a mental health problem.

When Kate was five years old, her mother had read bedtime stories with her and then tucked her in. Swaddled in kisses and covers, Kate had nestled in for the night....

A noise startled her. She clenched the covers and listened again. A light rain pinged off the roof. The wind was blowing. Thunder clapped.

The screeching came again. Her heart stuttered. That wasn't the storm. It sounded like a cat was crying. In pain. She had to do something. Save it.

Barefoot, she slipped from bed and tiptoed to the back door. But she hated the dark and the lightning zigzagging across the treetops, making her jump back from the door. She couldn't go outside alone. What if it was a wild animal in the backyard instead of a cat?

She ran to the window, pushed the curtain aside and peered out into the night. The moon was only a sliver tonight. A few stars glittered, just enough for her to see something by the back porch near her window. The crying grew louder.

She ran to her mommy's room and pushed the door open. "Mommy, I heard something. I think it's a cat outside. It might be hurt."

Mommy stood in front of the bathroom mirror rub-

bing face cream on her cheeks. "Are you sure it's not just the storm?"

"No, I heard crying," Kate whispered. "He's hurt and out there in the rain."

Mommy set the jar of cream on the counter then clasped Kate's hand and squeezed it, reassuring her with a smile. She loved her mommy so much. Mommy was always smiling and made everything all right. "Come on, we'll look together."

Together they rushed to the front door. Mommy paused and listened. Worry flickered in her eyes. Then she quickly opened the door and stepped out onto the porch.

More thunder clapped and lightning lit up the sky. Rain ran from the roof, pounding the ground by the porch and splattering mud everywhere.

Kate shivered, hanging on to Mommy's leg. Suddenly the thunder's rumble grew softer, and an eerie silence fell. A second later, Kate saw the bushes rustling by the steps.

"Over there." Kate pointed to the right side of the porch.

Mommy patted her shoulder. "Stay here, sweetie. "It's probably a stray cat trying to get out of the rain."

Kate clung to the porch railing as Mommy ran down the steps. Another streak of lightning flashed, and Kate saw her mommy stoop beside the stairs.

Her heart pounded with fear. What if she was too late to save the cat? Or what if something got Mommy?

A second later, Mommy stood. She wasn't holding a cat, though. It was the little girl next door, Macy. Macy *was shivering and shaking as she wrapped her arms around Kate's mommy's neck and sobbed into her chest.*

Kate rubbed her eyes to keep from crying, too. Poor Macy, she looked like a drowned rat.

"Come on, let's get you out of the rain," Mommy said.

Macy clung to Mommy as she carried her into the kitchen. "Get me a towel, Kate."

Kate raced to the drawer and grabbed a couple of drying cloths and handed them to her mommy, who wiped at the mud on Macy's knees and hands where she'd crawled beneath the steps for cover from the downpour.

Kate shivered as her mommy soothed Macy. Finally, when Macy stopped sobbing, Mommy lifted Macy's chin and looked at her face.

"Are you hurt anywhere, honey?" Mommy asked.

Macy's chin quivered, but she shook her head.

"What happened?" Mommy asked.

Macy looked down at her soaking clothes and her face turned red.

"It's okay, you can tell me," Mommy said. "Kate and I just want to be your friend." Mommy rubbed Macy's back. "Did you get locked out of the house?"

Macy ducked her head again, her voice a low pained whisper. "Mommy got mad and put me out. She told me I was too much trouble and I could sleep outside with the dogs tonight."

Kate gasped but her mommy kept soothing Macy. "Sweetheart, no little girl should sleep outside, much

*less in this weather. Is your mommy okay? Was some-
one else there?"*

"No one was there but her," Macy said on another
sob. "She just got mad at me. She does that sometimes
when she doesn't want me around. She says I'm tr...
ouble."

Kate barely held back a cry, but her mommy's warning look told her to stay quiet. That this was bad. Real
bad.

"Well, you can stay here tonight with me and Kate,
right, Kate?"

Kate nodded, her heart hurting. Mommy would never
make her go outside in the rain alone, much less sleep
outside. Macy didn't have a dog, either. The only one
nearby belonged to Big Rob the Butcher at the end of
the street. Big Rob and his dog snarled at you if you
got near either one of them.

"Let's get you in some dry pajamas." Mommy lifted
Macy, and Kate followed her to Kate's bedroom.

"She can wear some of yours, can't she, Kate?"

Kate's favorite pj's had flying unicorns on them, and
she'd never shared her clothes before. But Macy looked
like she needed some flying unicorns tonight, so she dug
them from her drawer and pushed them toward Macy.

"These are the bestest ones," Kate said. "They always bring me sweet dreams."

Macy changed in the bathroom, then Mommy
brought them both cookies in bed and Kate gave Macy
her stuffed puppy to sleep with. Then her mother sang
them songs until they both fell asleep.

The next morning, she heard her mommy raise her

voice for the first time ever. She had called Macy's
mother and they were having a talk.

Later she explained to Kate that Macy's mother was
sick and that illness caused her to do things that might
hurt Macy. From then on, it was their job to watch
over Macy.

A TREE BRANCH scraped the window outside, bringing
Kate back to the present. From then on, Kate and Macy
had been inseparable. Kate's mother had driven Macy
to school and back. They'd taken her to the park with
them and to the zoo and to movies. Macy spent the night
at her house more than her own.

But Macy rarely talked about that first night, or the
other times when her mother had thrown a fit, or why
Macy never invited Kate to play at her house.

Kate knew the reason. Her friend didn't have to say
the words out loud.

Kate loved her mother even more for taking Macy
in with no questions asked.

And then her mother had died and Macy had disappeared from her life, leaving an even bigger hole in
Kate's chest.

Kate walked over to the window. Smoke still seeped
into the sky. Riggs hadn't hesitated to rush out to help
battle the blaze. He could have gotten killed.

Maybe she was wrong about him.

It didn't matter. She'd lost Brynn and Macy and her
mother. She couldn't afford to let herself care about
someone else.

BY THE TIME Riggs reached Kate's, he'd decided Gretta might be responsible for the letter of blame to Kate. Gretta's father had owned an auto repair shop before he died. She could have learned enough from him to know how to cut a gas line.

He parked, then sent Stone a text relaying his theory. Maybe Stone could get the blasted woman's fingerprints or DNA for comparison in case they lifted some from the matchbook or car. Stone texted a reply that he would consider Riggs's suggestion.

Riggs scanned Kate's property, alert for trouble, as he walked up to the porch. The scent of smoke and burned wood lingered, but he didn't see anyone lurking around.

He wiped soot from his hands onto his pants and rang the doorbell. Seconds later, the sound of footsteps echoed from inside and then the lock turned.

He sucked in a breath as Kate opened the door. Her long hair spilled over her shoulders in sexy waves.

"Are you okay?" she asked in a raspy voice.

"Yeah. Are you?"

She nodded and gestured for him to come inside. Although he'd removed his firefighting equipment, his hair and skin held the smoky scent of where he'd been.

"We extinguished the blaze," he said. "But it burned at least a half mile of woods. Deputies and the fire department will monitor the area tonight to make sure the wind doesn't spark the fire back to life."

Kate rubbed her arms with her hands. "Was anyone hurt?"

"No. Thankfully, we didn't find casualties or anyone trapped or injured."

Kate heaved a sigh of relief. "Thank God. I was worried about you."

He arched a brow, surprised at her admission. "I know what I'm doing, Kate."

A soft smile flickered in her eyes. "Your job is still dangerous."

What was dangerous was the heat simmering between the two of them. He wanted nothing more right now than to pull Kate into his arms and hold her. To wipe that worry off her face with a mind-blowing kiss.

Her gaze locked with his and, for a second, he thought she might welcome that kiss.

Then she turned and walked over to her desk by the sliding-glass doors leading to her back deck, and he called himself all kinds of a fool.

"I made a list of students for Stone," she said. "Although I don't think any of them is violent enough to try to kill me."

Riggs didn't want to frighten her, but they couldn't bury their heads in the sand. Everyone had done that with Ned. Ignored the signs.

Then it was too late.

"We can't be too careful, Kate. Someone is playing a deadly game and he or she needs to be stopped."

Kate rubbed her arms with her hands to ward off the chill. "I can't believe this is happening."

"I know and I'm sorry. But I found an empty matchbook in the woods. It could have belonged to the person who set the fire."

"Or someone was smoking and accidentally dropped a cigarette or match."

"That's possible. Or they lit the match and intentionally threw it into the weeds to start the fire," Riggs said. "Woody is a smoker but he's still in a cell, so he didn't do it."

Kate shifted uncomfortably and looked back at the envelope on her desk.

"That the list of students?" he asked.

She murmured that it was.

"Any of them smokers?"

Kate sighed again. "Don Gaines. He was caught in the bathroom at school and outside behind the bleachers."

"You notified his folks?"

"Yes. But Don is all talk. He wouldn't have the guts to come after me."

"His sister was paralyzed because of that shooting, Kate. That had to have affected the entire family."

"I know, but—"

"Maybe you could talk to Brynn," he suggested.

Kate ran a hand through her hair, pushing it away from her forehead. "I can't suggest to Brynn that her brother is an arsonist. Besides, she and I haven't been close in years."

"Why is that? I thought you and Macy and Brynn were best friends."

A wave of sadness washed over her face. "We were. But that was a long time ago."

She didn't elaborate and he sensed the subject was closed.

Kate might not believe Don was dangerous. But the kid had an attitude.

And Riggs didn't trust him.

KATE COULD JUST imagine Brynn's reaction if she showed up tossing accusations at her little brother. And the mayor and his wife... Mrs. Gaines hated her already.

"Macy was with Stone at the scene of the fire tonight," Riggs said.

Kate lifted her head. "What was she doing there?"

"Stone asked her to look over his father's files. He hopes she'll find something he missed."

"That makes sense, I guess."

"She asked about you," Riggs said, his gaze scrutinizing her.

Tears blurred Kate's eyes and she blinked to stem them. Earlier, she'd been thinking about Macy and Macy's awful childhood, and how they'd been like sisters when they were young.

"She said she's going to clear out her mother's house and put it on the market while she's here," Riggs said.

Kate's heart squeezed. "I heard her mother was institutionalized."

"What happened between you two?" Riggs asked.

Kate clenched her hands by her sides, annoyed at his persistence. "Everything changed after the shooting. As soon as graduation was over, Macy just moved away." Without even saying goodbye.

Her abandonment had felt like a knife in Kate's gut at the time.

Her phone trilled, saving her from more questions,

and she rushed to answer it, although she had no idea who would be calling at this time of night. Maybe someone from the school council about the memorial.

"Hello?"

"Back off, Kate," a deep muffled voice growled, "or next time your fireman boyfriend won't be able to save you."

Cold fear seized Kate as the line went dead.

Chapter Twelve

Riggs narrowed his eyes as Kate hung up the phone. Her face had gone pasty white. "What's wrong, Kate?"

She sank onto her sofa and dropped her head into her hands.

Riggs gritted his teeth, walked over and joined her. She looked so upset that he wanted to take her in his arms and hold her. "Who was on the phone?"

"I don't know." She raked a trembling hand through her hair and looked up at him with a mixture of fear and confusion.

Riggs couldn't resist. He rubbed her back in slow circles to comfort her. "Talk to me, Kate. What exactly did he say?"

"The voice was muffled, so I couldn't tell if it was a man or a woman. But whoever it was said, 'Back off, Kate, or next time your fireman boyfriend won't be able to save you.'"

Riggs went cold inside. He didn't mind being called her boyfriend, but the fact that the caller knew he was there meant he was watching Kate. That he wanted to do more than scare her. And that she'd been the target of that fire.

"Did he say anything else?"

"No." Her chin quivered. "But he must be nearby, watching me."

Riggs muttered a curse as he rushed to the sliders overlooking the back yard. Shoulders rigid, he stepped outside and searched the darkness. Shadows flitted like dark soldiers in the night through the woods as the trees rustled and moved in the wind.

The caller implied he'd set that fire to get to Kate. That meant the same person who'd set it had tampered with her SUV.

Through the faint sliver of moonlight fighting its way through the fog and smoke, he searched the darkness for her stalker, but he didn't see anyone in the yard. Although a pair of binoculars could allow the perp to watch from afar.

Pulse jumping, Riggs raced to the front of the house. Through the window, he scanned the yard and street, searching for movement. A car, a match striking, or a cigarette glowing in the dark.

Kate moved up behind him. "Do you see anyone?"

The hair on the nape of his neck stood on end. "No. But he's out there somewhere." He sensed it.

His hand went to his belt. "I'll call Stone. He can put a trace on your phone. If this bastard calls back, maybe he can catch him and stop this madness."

Kate ran her fingers through her hair, untangling the strands as she sighed.

His heart stuttered with tenderness for her, and he

cupped her face in his hands. "Don't worry, Kate. He's not going to get to you."

Her eyes searched his, emotions flaring. "You don't owe my mother, Riggs. She helped you because she cared. That's who she was."

Yes, he did owe her. Other than his own mother, she was the first person who'd believed he wasn't stupid.

Still, he had to be honest with himself. He wasn't just there to repay a debt to Elaine McKendrick. He liked Kate.

Need and desire leaped inside him, and he leaned closer to her. Her breath quickened, a seed of longing in her expressive eyes.

He threaded his fingers through the soft tresses of her hair, hunger consuming him. "I'm not doing this for your mother."

Then he did what he'd been wanting to do forever. He closed his mouth over hers and kissed her.

KATE'S SELF-PROTECTIVE instincts whispered for her to run. That Riggs had the power to break her heart.

You're a fool to let him get close.

But at the moment, she didn't care. Ever since she was fifteen, she'd wondered what it would be like to taste him. To have him look at her the way he just had.

To feel his lips on hers and his arms around her.

Riggs didn't disappoint.

He swept her hair back with his fingers and deepened the kiss, teasing her lips apart with his tongue and delving inside as if he craved her taste just as she did his.

She lifted her hands, tunneled one into his thick hair,

and pulled him to her. He teased and explored, taking and giving, until she felt her knees go weak.

Then he caught her around her waist and cradled her against his body. His muscles pressed against her soft curves, teasing her with his masculinity. He mumbled her name on a throaty sigh and unbuttoned her blouse as he walked her backward toward the sofa.

Caught up in the moment, Kate clung to him and fell onto the plush cushions. Her head hit the pillow, her breathing ragged, and he caressed her cheek with his thumb again. Then he dipped his head and pressed tender kisses along her throat, lighting a trail of fire though her body.

That need suddenly sent a streak of terror through her.

"You're beautiful, Kate," he murmured.

Tears pricked her eyes as another memory surfaced. Another man, her college boyfriend, telling her she was beautiful and then laughing as he'd walked away after he'd screwed her.

She couldn't do this. Give in to this raging need for Riggs.

The passion in his eyes turned into a question. "Kate?"

"Stop," she whispered. "Please."

He searched her face, her eyes. Then he lifted his body from hers, pushed away from the sofa, and walked over to the sliding glass doors.

The sound of the doors opening made her regret her request, but she'd be foolish to ask him to come back.

Kate McKendrick was a practical kind of girl, not a love-struck teenager.

She quickly buttoned her blouse, humiliation climbing her neck as she realized how close she'd come to letting Riggs strip her naked on the couch.

Outside on the deck, he stood with his back to her, looking out into the woods, his body rigid, hands curled around the railing.

Fighting the urge to go to him and beg him to finish what they'd begun, she hurried into her bedroom and shut the door.

Riggs had promised not to let anyone hurt her.

But *he* could hurt her if she let down her defenses again.

RIGGS GRIPPED THE railing so tightly he thought the wood might splinter. What the hell had just happened?

He'd kissed Kate, that was what had happened. He'd kissed her and that kiss had been so damn hot he hadn't been able to stop himself. No, he could have stopped himself—he just hadn't wanted to.

So he'd kept going and one taste of her neck had made him crave more. And then, for God's sake, he'd unbuttoned her blouse, seen that scrap of red lace, and thought he'd die if he didn't have her.

Who knew sweet, tough, levelheaded Kate liked decadent underwear?

Her breasts…they were every bit as luscious-looking as he'd imagined.

And he had fantasized about them. When he was in

high school. When he'd seen her around town. In his sleep. After all, he was a red-blooded male.

And she was…exquisite.

You're a bastard, man. Kate was scared and you came onto her.

Of course she'd told him to stop. He'd practically mauled her.

Although, for a brief second, he'd felt passion between them as if it wasn't one-sided. As if Kate wanted him.

He hadn't imagined it, had he?

Forcing himself to take long, deep breaths, he wrangled his libido under control. The wind picked up, stirring the acrid scent of smoke and burned wood, a reminder of the reason he was at Kate's.

And of the phone call.

Dammit, he had to update Stone. Should have alerted him the minute Kate had told him about the threat.

He snagged his phone from his belt and punched Stone's number. "I came back to Kate's after I left the fire," Riggs said. "Where are you?"

"Just left the mayor's house. I stopped by to see if Don Gaines was home."

Riggs's pulse quickened. "Was he?"

"He'd just gotten in," Riggs said. "Mayor didn't like my questions, but Don smelled like smoke, and had mud on his sneakers."

"Where did he say he'd been?"

"Out with some buddies. I'll call them and verify his story when I return to the station. Mr. Gaines refused to let Don give me a DNA sample or his prints, so I'm requesting a warrant."

"While you're at it, get one for his cell phone."

"What's up?" Stone asked.

Riggs explained about the phone call. "This bastard is stalking her, Stone."

Stone mumbled a curse. "Poor Kate. I bet she's completely unraveled."

Kate unraveled? He was the one coming unraveled. "She was shaken," Riggs admitted. "She gave permission for you to put a trace on her cell in case the caller phones again."

"On it." He hunched his shoulders. "Macy's been reviewing Dad's old files. She plans to connect with our former classmates at the picnic tomorrow. Maybe time has mellowed everyone and, if someone did know something, he or she is ready to talk."

Kate would probably be front and center at the picnic. So might the person threatening her.

He bit back a curse. He wanted her tucked away safe and sound.

In his bed.

Not going to happen, man.

"Maybe Billy will show up," Stone said.

"Maybe." Twigs snapped from somewhere in the distance and a tree branch splintered and sailed to the ground. Riggs craned his neck to search the area again. "He may be lurking nearby." That would be Billy's style.

Stone nodded. "If he's escalating, he might make a mistake and tip his hand in public."

"We can hope."

Stone hung up, then the slider doors squeaked open. Riggs steeled himself against reacting…or reaching for Kate again.

The scent of her lavender bodywash wafted to him, aromatic and feminine in contrast to the thick, cloying, smoky odor.

"Riggs, I—"

"Go to bed, Kate."

Her raspy breath punctuated the air, torturing him. "W-we should talk," she said in a low whisper.

Hell, no. Not with her standing in the fading moonlight with her hair spilling around her shoulders and the image of that red lacy bra fresh in his mind. "There's nothing to talk about. You wanted to stop and we did. You can lock the door if you're afraid of me."

She took a step toward him. "I'm not afraid," Kate breathed.

But she was. Fear glittered in her eyes.

That hurt more than if she'd physically hit him. "I told you I'd protect you, and I will. I'll sleep on the couch and I won't bother you again."

"Riggs—"

"Please, Kate. Go. To. Bed."

His gruff voice must have gotten to her because she turned and disappeared inside the house. A minute later, he heard her bedroom door close.

Good, she was out of sight. Safe.

Riggs was the one in danger of losing himself in her sweet body and eyes.

But he needed to stop any fantasies of having Kate. He had to stay focused and protect her.

He'd lost a friend in the shooting and two more in a fire last year. The sound of that warehouse collapsing, trapping two of his partners who'd gone in to save innocents, haunted him every night. Tony Almono and Will Elrod, both over six feet and strong as oxen. But not strong enough to survive an inferno or the burning rubble that had covered them in flames and hot gas.

Hell, he used to be fun-loving and cocky. But he'd seen too many good people get killed to forget that death came for everybody at some time.

Kate was too good a person for it to come for her just yet.

KATE WAS AS shaken by the kiss with Riggs as she was the fire. His comment about Macy reviewing the original case files from the shooting investigation played through her head as she readied for bed.

Why had Macy left town without saying goodbye?

Why did you let the distance between you two go on for so long...? You could have tried harder to reach out to her. Harder to get her to forgive you. Harder to keep her in your life.

But Kate had been too embroiled in her own grief to think about anyone except herself.

She punched her pillow in frustration. As a member of the planning committee, Amy had kept a list of all the addresses and phone numbers for the alumni. Kate rose from bed, booted up her computer and searched the list until she found Macy's.

Even if her former best friend didn't want to reconcile, she at least owed her an apology for how she'd acted fifteen years ago. Macy had never known how to reach out for help, and if she'd needed it, would have tried to handle things on her own, just as she had as a kid.

With the new school, Kate hoped for a new beginning. Maybe she needed a new one with Macy.

Still, her hand trembled slightly as she crawled back into bed and pressed Macy's number.

The phone rang four times then her voice mail picked up. "This is Special Agent Macy Stark. Please leave a message with your number and I'll get back to you as soon as I can."

Kate tensed. What she had to say needed to be said in person, not on a message machine. Macy knew where she lived and could come by, but she hadn't. Maybe she was screening her calls and didn't want to talk.

Biting her lip, she pressed End Call without leaving a message. She'd try again later. Or maybe she'd see Macy at one of the reunion events and they could talk.

But worry knotted her stomach as Kate closed her eyes, and memories of the shooting returned to haunt her....

THE BELL HAD RUNG, signaling time to change to third period, when Ned had flown into a rage. Kate and Macy and Brynn had just met at their lockers, chatting about nothing, when the first bullet was fired.

Their lockers were directly across from Kate's mother's classroom. Riggs had just come out, and she and Macy turned to head into English class while Brynn had Trig.

But screams erupted as the bullets began to ping off the lockers and victims began to fall.

Kate's mother stepped out and raised a hand to try to convince Ned to put down the gun. Just as she did, Ned waved the gun. Macy froze, her eyes wide with terror, then Kate heard the sound of the gun going off.

Shock immobilized her as she watched Riggs get hit and fall, blood spurting from his leg as he doubled over in pain. Brynn and the others began to run into classrooms, some kids pushing and shoving to get out of the line of fire.

Ned looked straight at Kate then aimed his weapon at Macy. Then it all happened so quickly that Kate forgot the sequence of events. All she remembered was Macy's scream, the sound of the bullet and then her mother collapsing onto the floor, blood soaking her blouse.

Chapter Thirteen

Riggs's taste still lingered on Kate's lips when she stirred from sleep the next morning, thankfully wiping away some of the bitter taste of the memories that had followed her to bed.

Between the shooting, the recent threats, that unsettling moment with Riggs, and knowing he was sleeping on her couch only a few feet away from her bed, she'd tossed and turned for hours. Finally, when she'd drifted to sleep, instead of nightmares of the shooting years ago, the car fire, or the fire in the woods, she'd dreamed of making love with Riggs.

Her body ached from unsated desire.

But she'd made the right choice by pulling away from Riggs. To her, making love meant more than a physical connection. She couldn't get naked with Riggs without involving her heart. And no doubt Riggs would be turned off by a clingy woman.

Resolve set in. Today it was back to business. She had meetings about the plans for the memorial, and she didn't intend to allow anyone to stand in the way.

She hurriedly showered and dressed in a loose skirt and blouse, then went into the kitchen to make coffee.

Riggs had beaten her to the task, though. He'd also used her guest bath to clean up and was wearing a fresh blue shirt and jeans that hugged his muscular butt and thighs.

A wave of longing washed over her. Lord help her, she had to get a grip.

Lifting her chin, she strode into the kitchen and poured herself a mug of coffee. For a second, she simply inhaled the aroma, allowing it to jump-start her brain. During the school year, she had to be up early and didn't have time to linger over coffee. Although she still worked several weeks during the summer, she made it a point to savor the morning ritual.

Riggs stared out into the woods, as he had been doing the night before when she'd gone to bed. She realized he was on the phone when he lowered it from his ear and clipped it to his belt.

Curious to learn if he had news, she opened the sliders and stepped onto the deck. The temperature seemed warmer today, although a slight breeze stirred the trees and brought the acrid scent of burned leaves, trees and ash. Cloud cover cast shadows across the land, making it look eerie and desolate in the gray light.

Riggs's big body stiffened as he slowly faced her. His dark brows were furrowed into a frown, his jaw tight. He took a long, slow sip of his coffee. His eyes were smoldering—with memories of the night before and… anger? Disappointment?

Kate swallowed hard to make her voice work and

attempted to banish the memory of his lips on hers. "Good morning."

A dark intensity radiated from him. "Morning, Kate."

The gruff way he murmured her name made her touch her lips with her fingers. A mistake. Riggs's eyes followed the movement.

Irritated with herself, she sank onto the glider to sip her coffee. "Did you sleep?" she asked.

"Some."

"I'm sorry," Kate said.

"No sweat. Odd hours go with my job. I'm used to it." He leaned his back against the railing. "Stone called about the phone. Looks like the caller used a burner phone. Makes it damn near impossible to trace."

"That figures." Kate glanced out into the woods. Noises and voices broke the early morning serenity of the mountains.

"The crime techs came back at first light to search for forensics," Riggs explained. "Stone said he stopped by the mayor's house last night to get his son's prints for comparison, but Don wasn't home. I have an idea of how to obtain it. Do you keep a record of the students' locker assignments?"

"Yes," Kate said. "But dozens of kids touch the lockers when they're hanging out between classes."

"True. But he's probably the only one who touched the interior space. Maybe we'll get lucky and he left his prints or DNA inside somewhere."

Kate hated to point suspicion toward Brynn's brother.

But if he had set that fire, someone could have been hurt, and she couldn't bury her head in the sand.

A HALF HOUR LATER, Riggs followed Kate to the school. Stone had liked his plan for obtaining Don's prints and agreed to meet them. Kate could hand off the list then.

Over a quick breakfast, Riggs had kept the conversation focused on the investigation and avoided discussing the evening before. Kate had made it perfectly clear she didn't want him.

Still, the devil must be punishing him because he'd dreamed about her all night. Crazy dreams of cuddling on Sunday mornings. Watching the news together. Enjoying long walks and bike rides. Cooking dinner together. Making homemade pasta.

Homemade pasta for cripes' sake. He'd seen Kate's machine on the counter. But he was a meat-and-potatoes man.

Dammit.

He parked in front of the school and cursed at the sight of the graffiti on the wall. Vandalizing a building was a crime, but petty compared to arson or attempted murder. Were these crimes being committed by the same person?

The tone of the threats suggested they were.

Stone pulled in just after him. Riggs exited his truck and waited on Stone, giving Kate the space she needed. This was her work: the new school project, her baby.

He wanted to make it happen for her and for the town.

"Are you going to the picnic today?" Stone asked.

There were only a handful of former classmates Riggs gave one iota about seeing. "If Kate goes, I am."

"Thanks for keeping an eye out for her," Stone said.

Hell, he'd do it even if Stone hadn't asked.

Stone scratched his chin as they walked up to the front of the building. "What if there's more to the threats against Kate than just someone being upset about the demolition of the old school?"

"I've been thinking about that, too. If Ned had an accomplice, that person has gotten off scot-free for years." Riggs opened the front door and stepped inside the school. "He or she sure as hell wouldn't want to be exposed now. And with everyone rehashing what happened, it would make an accomplice afraid of being exposed."

"Exactly."

"Did you talk to Ned's parents?"

"I spoke to Mr. Hodgkins. He and his wife are still out of town. And, no surprise, he's bitter. I think they still blame themselves for what happened, too."

Riggs made a low sound in his throat. "I can understand that."

"He was adamant that he and his wife would never set foot back in Briar Ridge. They support the new building, though, said they wanted the place where their son murdered innocent kids to be wiped off the map."

Who could blame them? "I can't imagine living with the fact that your own child killed his classmates."

"Yeah, another kind of hell."

Hell was right. Riggs had watched Ned gun down another classmate before he'd shot him. Then he'd aimed his gun at Macy and at Kate. He'd never forget the terror on their faces or the screams that echoed up and down the halls. Doors slamming. Students running for their lives. Taking cover anywhere they could. Bashing windows just to jump outside and escape.

Then the gun firing again. He'd stared in helpless shock, blood soaking him, and expected Kate or Macy to fall beside him. But Mrs. McKendrick had stepped in the way and saved their lives.

Then the sirens, Ned running, the police storming in. Crying all around him, terrified screams and rescue workers rushing in to take care of the injured and dead.

"There's Kate," Stone said, pushing away Riggs's thoughts of the painful past.

Kate motioned them over. When Riggs stepped further inside, it struck him how empty the building felt. Bare walls. Furniture and posters and billboards gone. No sounds of teens talking and laughing, or music, or the bell ringing.

Students wouldn't be returning here in the fall or ever again.

Pleasant memories of his own years at Briar Ridge drifted back. Football rallies, soccer games, homecoming and prom.

His nervous stomach over tests he was afraid he wouldn't pass.

Then that horrible day all over again.

"Here's the list," Kate said, interrupting his thoughts again.

Riggs was glad the building would be gone soon. Maybe one day they'd all begin to forget.

"Honestly, Stone, I can't see any of these kids trying to kill me," Kate said as she handed Stone an envelope. "None of the infractions were serious."

"Maybe, maybe not. But I'll check them out just in case." He paused. "Is Don Gaines on the list?"

Kate shifted from one foot to the other, her fingers stroking the strap of her bag. "Yes. He was caught smoking in the bathroom and outside. But—"

"Just show me his locker," Stone said flatly.

Kate gestured to the hall leading toward the science wing. "I don't want to accuse Don of something unless you have definitive proof," Kate said as they walked. "The Gaines family suffered enough after the shooting."

A muscle twitched in Riggs's jaw. So like Kate to think about helping the kid instead of being angry with him.

"Look at this way, Kate," Stone said calmly. "Lifting his prints may clear him and we can cross him off the suspect list."

Riggs touched Kate's arm. "Besides, if the prints from the locker don't match the one on the matchbook, Don and his family never have to know you did this."

Kate waffled. "I suppose that's true."

Resigned, Kate stopped at a set of lockers near the exit to the breezeway that connected the main building to the gym. Don had been in the science lab—to retrieve his phone, he'd claimed—around the same time the threat had been graffitied on the outside wall. Don's locker was near the exit closest to the gym.

Kate inserted a master key and opened the locker.

Stone indicated for her not to touch anything while he yanked on latex gloves to search the interior.

No books. Trash from a candy bar wrapper. Two foil packs of condoms. A nude picture from a porn magazine.

Riggs shook his head, surprised the kid had left the picture behind. Then again, with his money, Don probably had a stash of girly magazines in his room. And internet porn was so easily accessible, he might have a mile-long list of sites he frequented.

Stone bagged each of the items. Just as he lifted the picture, Riggs spotted a matchbook on the bottom of the locker.

A matchbook from Smokehouse Barbecue.

KATE FOLDED HER ARMS. "The matches—"

"Are from the same place as the matchbook I found in the woods last night," Riggs said.

She bit her bottom lip. "That doesn't mean Don set the fire. Anyone could have picked up a book of matches from Smokehouse Barbecue."

"True, but he still shouldn't have matches at school," Stone said. "Hopefully we can lift prints and compare."

Footsteps echoed from down the hall, and Kate checked her watch as Jimmy appeared. His limp seemed more pronounced today and he looked tired, his wiry hair sticking out, the wrinkles around his eyes more prominent, as if he hadn't been sleeping well. "Ms. McKendrick, there's some folks here from the town council, say they're supposed to meet with you. Amy Turner is already in your office."

"Thanks, Jimmy. Tell them I'll be right there." She tilted her head at the two men. "I have to go. We need to finalize details for the memorial."

"We're right behind you," Riggs said.

Kate headed down the hall, Riggs beside her, Stone on their heels.

"Are you going to the picnic?" Riggs asked.

They stopped in front of the door to her office. "I have to show up. I helped organize these events. I'd hoped a reunion might help mend friendships." She wished she could mend her own with Macy and Brynn. If Don Gaines turned out to be the one threatening her, she would only drive a wedge deeper between her and Brynn.

"I'll swing back by and pick you up after your meeting," Riggs offered.

"Thanks, but I'll drive. I have an errand to do on the way."

"I could help."

Kate shook her head. "The memorial is supposed to be a surprise. Besides, I'm just going to the frame shop in town. There will be dozens of people around."

Stone cleared his throat. "I need to drop this stuff at the lab. You coming, Riggs?"

Riggs shrugged. "Yeah."

Kate spotted the mayor entering the building. His gray eyes cut to Stone.

"Sheriff?" Mayor Gaines raised a brow. "What are you doing here?"

Kate tensed, but Stone didn't miss a beat. "We're investigating that graffiti outside. Someone also tampered with Kate's car, so I have to take the threat against her seriously."

"Last night, someone also set a fire in the woods behind her house," Riggs added. "Kate may have been a target."

The mayor coughed. "I'm well aware of the fire." He pierced Stone with a disapproving look, although Stone let it roll off his back. Stone was not into politics—he was known for being fair and out for justice. He also wouldn't let anyone push him around.

"I hope you find out who's doing this," the mayor continued. "Kate is a valuable member of the community."

"Yes, she is," Stone agreed.

"I can assure you my son was not involved." The mayor's cheeks turned ruddy. "I talked to him after you left, Sheriff. I'm not proud of it, but he and his friends were buying weed last night. That's the reason he wasn't home." He made a guttural sound in his throat. "I intend to see that he gets the help he needs."

"That's wise," Kate said, proud of the mayor for owning his son's problem. Many parents lived in denial.

Stone gave the mayor a deadpan look. "I'm not pointing a finger at anyone yet," Stone said. "Just gathering evidence to see where it leads us."

Amy poked her head into the hallway from Kate's office. "I'm here, Kate."

"We should get started on the meeting." Kate gestured toward the mayor. "Are you ready?"

He nodded and followed Amy as she retreated to

Kate's office. Riggs caught Kate's arm before she left. "Don't let him intimidate you."

"Don't worry. I don't intend to."

He squeezed her arm. "Call me if you need me."

Nerves gathered in her stomach. She wouldn't call. She couldn't afford to need him. She had to stand on her own, just as she always had.

TWO HOURS LATER, storm clouds hovered over the park, threatening to ruin the reunion picnic. To Riggs's surprise, though, the inclement weather hadn't deterred the Briar Ridge High graduates from showing up. In fact, some former classmates seemed to be excited over reconnecting with past alumni. Even now, old friends were introducing their families and kids were running and playing on the playground.

Without realizing it, Kate's efforts might already be working its healing magic. Their senior year had been so fraught with tension and grief that perhaps everyone had needed to come back together to prove they'd survived.

Although with the threats against Kate, Riggs's senses were honed. Anyone at the reunion could have information about Ned's accomplice. Hell, the accomplice could be hiding in plain sight.

Billy Hodgkins ranked at the top of his suspect list. He could have helped his brother and was now panicked that his part in the mass shooting might be revealed.

Don Gaines couldn't have been an accomplice fifteen years ago, but he might be traumatized enough by what had happened to his sister to threaten Kate now.

Riggs stood at the edge of the pavilion, scrutinizing the group. Some faces he recognized instantly. Others had changed or were only blips in his memory because they'd run in different circles.

His two friends, Jay Lakewood and Duke Eastman, were talking to Ellie Kane and Vera Long, former cheerleaders. Stone's brother Mickey was sitting on a park bench with Cassidy Fulton.

That was odd. He didn't think the two were friendly. Cassidy certainly wasn't romantically interested in a man with a disability—as she'd stressed when Riggs had been in rehab for his leg.

But…a thought suddenly occurred to him. Cassidy had never revealed the name of her baby's father. What if Mickey was Roy's father? Before the shooting, Mickey had been a wild party guy.

Losing his sight had shattered his dreams of playing football in college, although he seemed to have found his artistic side. Now he played the guitar and sang in a local honky-tonk. From what Riggs had heard, Mickey was talented and was beginning to write his own music.

Cara Winthrop's little sister Evie was in deep conversation with Rae Lynn Porter. Cara had been Ned's third victim; he'd shot her five times.

He didn't remember much about Rae Lynn, except she'd been a Goth girl. She'd lost the dramatic look of the Goth attire now, but her jet-black hair still contrasted sharply with her milky-white skin, and tattoos snaked up and down her arms.

Gretta sauntered through the park, stopping to chat as she worked the crowd. Although, judging from the way classmates cut her out of their conversations, no one trusted her. Hell, how could they forget how sneaky she'd been? How she'd blurted out personal secrets to the entire school?

A van pulled up and parked, and he recognized Brynn's vehicle, which had been adapted to accommodate her wheelchair. A driver got out, went around to the side, opened the door, retrieved Brynn's chair and helped her into it.

Riggs made himself look away and not stare. He *was* one of the lucky ones. PT had restored his ability to walk so he hadn't been left permanently disabled. Mrs. Gaines, he knew, had always been overbearing and smothering. He couldn't imagine what Brynn's life was like under her roof.

The wind picked up, hurling leaves across the park. Another car sounded, and Kate drove up in her rental SUV. Just as she got out, Billy Hodgkins jumped from a red sports car and cornered her by the Escape. Billy looked upset, his hands swinging wildly, his hair stringy and matted with sweat.

Anger knotted Riggs's stomach and he sprinted toward them.

Chapter Fourteen

Kate pressed herself against the car as Billy Hodgkins lurched at her.

Behind them in the park, former classmates and alumni were mingling and socializing, enjoying refreshments and music. Her heart gave a pang at the sight of the babies and children.

Right now, though, they seemed a million miles away.

"We need to talk." The dark scowl on Billy's face reminded her of the day he'd cornered her at the cemetery.

She tried to maneuver past him, but he trapped her against the car by planting both hands on the hood. The back of her thighs hit the front bumper.

The instructor in the self-defense class she'd taken in college emphasized not to show fear. Or to look vulnerable. To emit an air of self-confidence.

Lifting her chin in a show of bravado, she braced herself for a physical attack.

"Kate, listen to me," he said in a deep voice.

"Move out of my way, Billy." Kate used both hands to push him away and he stumbled backward. But before she made it two feet, he grabbed her arm.

She gave a pointed look to where his fingers held her a little too tightly and then spoke through clenched teeth. "Let go of me."

"You keep running from me and won't listen." Billy's voice took on a shrill edge. "You have to hear me out."

"She doesn't have to do anything," Riggs's deep voice boomed with authority as he walked up behind Billy. "And if you know what's good for you, Billy, you'll take your hands off of the lady like she asked."

A strand of Billy's shaggy hair fell across one eye, adding to his sinister look. "Back off, Riggs. This is none of your business. It's between me and Kate."

Riggs slapped a hand on Billy's shoulder and dug his fingers into the man's skin. "I'm making it my business. Now step away from Kate."

"Kate, listen," Billy cried. "I just need five minutes."

"Back. Away." A threat underlay Riggs's commanding tone.

A shiver rippled through Kate at the menacing look in Billy's eyes. But he released her arm, raised his hands in a surrender gesture and stepped back.

"What's going on?" This time Stone appeared, hands on his hips as he traced his fingers over his gun.

"I just wanted to talk to Kate," Billy barked. "But Benford jumped on me like a mad dog."

Riggs crossed his arms and spread his feet, an intimidating stance. "If you have anything to say to Kate, you can say it in front of us."

"Forget it." Billy cursed and started to walk away.

Stone blocked his retreat, his height towering over Billy as he looked down at him.

"What the hell?" Billy said. "I thought this was supposed to be a damn reunion. A chance to get back together with old friends."

"You were never friends with Kate," Riggs snarled.

"Neither were you." Billy hooked a thumb toward Kate. "Sheriff, Kate organized this shindig. You gonna stop everyone who wants to talk to her?"

"Anyone who's viewed as a threat," Stone said bluntly.

"Wait just a minute," Billy snarled. "Just because my brother did a stupid thing doesn't mean—"

"This is not about your brother, at least not directly," Stone interjected. "It's about the fact that someone has been threatening Kate and sabotaged her car."

Billy's eyes darted from Stone to Kate. "You think that was me?"

"We know you blame Kate for your brother's death," Riggs said in a cold tone. "The publicity for the new school and demolition of the old building must have triggered traumatic memories for you."

"Yeah, hell, it did. People ran my folks out of town. They had to change their names because the press made our lives a nightmare." He pounded his hand over his chest. "Did you know they received hate mail? Death threats? That people threw rocks in their living room and someone set fire to my father's hardware store?"

Kate had been so grief stricken from losing her mother and traumatized from witnessing the bloody massacre of her friends that the world had blurred. She had no idea the pain and suffering Ned's family had endured.

"I'm sorry, Billy," Kate said, sympathy lacing her voice.

Pain wrenched Billy's face.

"My father documented what happened," Stone added. "It must have been hell for your family, Billy. And for you." He paused. "All the more reason you might retaliate against the town now."

Confusion marred Billy's face. He seemed thrown off by their acknowledgment of his family's suffering.

"Kate is working to help the town revive the love we once shared and to make a better place for our children," Riggs said. "Blaming her is wrong."

"I didn't attack her," Billy snapped.

"Where were you last night?" Stone asked.

Billy's right eye twitched. "None of your business."

Stone tapped his badge. "As a matter of fact, it is. You can either answer my questions here or down at the station."

Billy shifted and yanked up his baggy jeans, which were sliding down over his hips and barrel belly. "I had dinner at a place outside of town."

"What place?" Stone asked.

"Pie in the Sky. It's across from the Lazy Dog Motel."

Stone tilted his head to the side. "Can anyone verify you were there?"

"Waitress," Billy said with a toothy grin.

Stone didn't find humor in it and neither did Riggs.

"Do you ever go to Smokehouse Barbecue?" Stone asked.

Billy shrugged. "A time or two. Most everyone in town does. Why do you want to know about that place?"

"Because someone set fire to the woods behind

Kate's house," Stone said. "And we found a pack of matches at the scene."

Billy's face paled. "I see what you're doing." He motioned at the crowd in the park. "Half the people out there are against tearing down the old school, but because it was my brother who shot it up, you're going to railroad me to jail for something I didn't do."

"I'm not railroading anyone," Stone said coldly. "But my job is to protect the citizens in Briar Ridge."

Billy raised his head in a defiant gesture. "You don't have anything on me because there's nothing to get. Now, I'm out of here." He gave them a go-to-hell look then stormed away.

"Let me grab my fingerprint kit," Stone said. "Billy's prints should be on the hood of your car, Kate. We'll see if his match the ones on that matchbook."

"I CAN'T BELIEVE the nerve of that guy," Riggs muttered as Billy roared from the parking lot.

Kate shrugged. "His family suffered. Maybe I should have listened to what he had to say."

Riggs gently turned Kate to look at him. "You don't owe that bastard anything. You did not cause his brother to kill our classmates or your mother, and you certainly don't have to put up with his bullying tactics."

Stone returned with his fingerprint kit, and Riggs gestured at the crowd. People had brought lounge chairs and picnic baskets, and old friends were getting reacquainted, playing Frisbee and football.

"We should mingle," he told Kate.

"Yeah, I guess we should."

Although she didn't sound thrilled at the idea.

How could she be excited or relaxed when the person who'd tried to kill her might be in the crowd?

For the next half hour, they talked to former classmates. Riggs kept his ears and eyes peeled for anyone acting suspiciously. Two girls he'd once dated flirted with him, but they no longer made his pulse jump like they had when he was sixteen.

Not like Kate did now.

He grabbed a bottle of water while Kate chatted with friends from the yearbook staff. Jay approached him with an eyebrow raise.

"Something going on with you and Kate?" Jay asked.

Riggs hesitated, maybe a fraction of a second too long. "I just don't want to see her get hurt."

"Uh-huh."

Riggs shifted and spotted Macy at the far end of the park, deep in conversation with another classmate, Trey Cushing. He'd heard the two of them had married.

"Keep telling yourself that," Jay said. "From what I've seen, you've got it bad for her."

Riggs heaved a weary breath and angled himself toward Jay so no one could overhear the conversation. "Fat lot of good it'll do. She still sees me as the player I used to be. That and the thing with Cassidy…"

"You could correct her, you know."

Riggs shrugged. "Maybe I will. If the subject comes up."

A frown tugged at Jay's mouth. "What's holding you back? I've never known you to be shy around a woman."

Riggs chuckled. "She's different." He rolled his shoulders. "Besides, why are you giving advice? Do you have a significant other I don't know about? Fiancée? Wife?"

Jay's smile faded. "I move around too much with the job."

"Excuses, excuses," Riggs said wryly.

This time Jay was the one who looked sheepish. "Guess we're both chicken when it comes to matters of the heart."

Turning around, they spotted Gretta stalking through a crowd of their classmates. "Speaking of dangerous women, run."

They both laughed, but their laughter died when Brynn Gaines wheeled her way down the hill to join the crowd. Gretta darted up beside her, her camera poised as she photographed Brynn's struggle over the rough patchy ground.

"That stupid witch," Jay said. "I'm going to rescue Brynn."

Jay strode off as if on a mission. He was going to have to hurry. Brynn had paused to reposition her chair, and Gretta caught up with her. She blocked Brynn's way and seemed relentless in firing questions at her.

Questions that, from Riggs's position, seemed to upset Brynn.

Speaking of trouble, Cassidy Fulton sashayed toward him.

Riggs steeled himself against a reaction. With her dyed-blond hair, low-cut top and shorts up her rear, Cassidy had been a hell-raiser in high school. She'd also used him and then tossed him aside like trash. Her cruel comments about his injury had shattered the remnants of his self-esteem at the time.

"Riggs." Cassidy fluttered her eyelashes at him as if the past didn't exist and he wouldn't remember what she'd done. "I heard you came to the rescue when Kate's car exploded."

"Just doing my job."

"Is someone really trying to kill her?" Cassidy asked.

He narrowed his eyes. "Where did you hear that?"

"Small town, word gets around."

Didn't he know it? "How's your son?"

A tiny seed of irritation flickered in her eyes. "Fine."

"Did his father ever step up?"

Any sign of friendliness fizzled out as quickly as a flame being doused by water.

"My son and his father are none of your business— or anyone else's." With a huff, Cassidy stormed away.

Riggs shrugged off her dismissal. He felt for the boy. Maybe he should reach out.

Kate's face caught his attention across the lawn, and he noticed her watching him, her face set in a deep frown.

He wanted to win her trust, for her to see him as a stand-up guy.

Dammit. But talking to the woman he'd supposedly impregnated and abandoned had just accomplished the opposite.

KATE SILENTLY CHIDED herself for watching Riggs and Cassidy. If Riggs wanted to talk to Cassidy or to sleep with her, he was free to do so.

So why was her heart hammering out of her chest with jealousy?

Riggs had a past with Cassidy. A child.

No one could change that.

When whoever was threatening her was caught and the activities surrounding the reunion and dedication for the new school were over, things would return to normal.

Riggs would resume his life—without her.

Her heart gave a pang.

Voices on the hill echoed loudly. Brynn… She was talking to Gretta. Only, Brynn looked upset.

Kate started up the hill to see if Gretta was harassing Brynn, but Jay approached them and lit into her.

Loud voices to the right made her halt in her tracks.

She pivoted and strained to see what the commotion was about, then spotted Macy standing with Trey Cushing. They were having a heated argument, though she couldn't hear what it was about.

Kate had never liked Trey. He'd been pushy with the girls.

On graduation night, she'd seen Macy and Trey leave together. Another blow—Kate thought she and Brynn and Macy would be celebrating together.

Instead, her friends had gone their separate ways.

The argument intensified and Trey leaned into Macy, his face contorted in rage. Macy shook her head and backed away as if to leave.

But Trey clutched Macy's wrist and yanked her to him.

Kate tensed. Macy was an FBI agent and could take care of herself. Although, as tough as Macy appeared,

Kate knew a vulnerable side lay beneath the surface. The side that had led them to become friends when Macy was five and needed help.

A side Macy didn't show to anyone.

Freeing herself from his grasp, Macy planted both hands on Trey's chest and pushed him back. He spit out a string of obscenities.

Wanting to reassure Macy that she still had her back, Kate veered toward them.

"Leave her alone," Kate said sharply.

Trey swung toward her, resentment and rage darkening his already vile expression. "Stay the hell out of our business, Kate."

Riggs's comments about Billy being a bully echoed in her head. Trey was a bully, too. "Trey, why don't you take a walk and calm down?"

Macy cut her eyes toward Kate. "Leave us alone, Kate. I've got this."

Her sharp tone made Kate's stomach clench and drove home the truth of the distance between them.

Suddenly, Kate felt overwhelmed. She was tired of fighting everyone on the school. Tired of being afraid. Tired of...being alone.

Still, she believed wholeheartedly that what she was doing for Briar Ridge was right, and she would see the school project through. Tomorrow.

Today she needed a break.

Battling tears, she rushed to her rental SUV, jumped in and drove straight to her house.

Her phone was ringing as she let herself in and

switched off the alarm. Riggs's name appeared on the Caller ID.

She let the phone roll to voice mail, poured herself a glass of wine and was just about to carry it to the back porch when the doorbell rang. Shoulders knotted with nerves, she checked the security camera. Riggs.

He looked worried. Maybe angry. And so sexy that she wanted to fall into his arms.

"Kate, open up." The doorbell rang again, followed by a loud knock. "Kate, please. I have to know you're okay."

She steeled herself against his sex appeal as she opened the door. "I'm fine, Riggs, you didn't have to come."

"Yes, I did. When you left the picnic so abruptly, I was worried something had happened."

He did sound worried, and a little bit angry. "I'm sorry," Kate said. "You were busy, and I was ready to leave." *And I couldn't stand seeing you with Cassidy.*

"Then you should have come and gotten me." Riggs strode past her into the room, his breathing heavy. "I was worried to death."

Kate's heart squeezed. "I'm okay—" Her voice died as something crashed through the sliding-glass doors.

Glass shattered. Then there was a popping sound and smoke began to pour into the room.

Chapter Fifteen

Riggs cursed. "Come on, Kate, we have to get out of here!" He pulled her through the front door onto the porch then down the steps to the lawn.

They ran to a large tree far away from the porch and Riggs shoved his phone into Kate's hands. "Call 9-1-1. I'm going to see if the bomber is still around."

Kate stabbed at the numbers while he scanned the street and front of the property. No one lurking nearby. No stray cars.

He raced around the side of the house toward the back. Whoever'd tossed the pipe bomb had to have been close by. Had to have climbed the steps to get the bomb through those sliders.

Glancing up at the deck, he saw it was empty. Smoke seeped through the broken glass, filling the deck and swirling upward in the wind.

Pivoting, he surveyed the back property. The area beneath the deck. Then the woods. Dammit, nothing.

Leaves rustled and trees swayed in the wind. The scent of burned wood from the forest fire still clung to the air. He walked along the trees lining Kate's property, searching the shadows.

A slight movement to the right. He stood frozen, listening, watching. A minute later, a deer scampered through the brush.

The sound of a car engine rumbled then tires squealed. Whoever had tossed that pipe bomb could have woven through the woods to the street farther down.

Riggs jogged up the incline and crossed the yard. Just as he made it to the road, the tail end of a car disappeared around the corner. He broke into a sprint, straining to get a read on the license plate, but the dark clouds shaded the remaining daylight, and the car was too fast.

The sound of a siren wailed from the opposite direction, then another. Riggs rushed back to check on Kate. A fire engine roared to a stop in the drive, followed by Stone's squad car.

Riggs darted toward the tree and found Kate looking shell-shocked.

"Are you okay?" he asked as he stopped in front of her.

"First the car fire, then the woods and now this." Her eyes glittered with anger and shock. "I want to know who's doing this."

"We'll find out." Riggs squeezed her arm. "Let me talk to Stone and the fire crew." He joined Stone and Brian where Brian was issuing orders as the crew began to tackle the blaze inside.

"What happened?" Stone asked.

"Someone threw a pipe bomb through the sliding-glass doors." Riggs raked a hand through his hair. "Kate and I ran out. I looked around back. Didn't see anyone, but I heard a car down the way, tires squealing. By the time I made it to the road, the car flew around the corner and disappeared."

"We'll contain the fire," Brian assured him as he and another firefighter geared-up, then rushed into the house.

"Did you see what kind of car it was?" Stone asked. "Get a license plate?"

"No." Riggs clenched his hands in frustration. "Dammit, Stone, Kate could have been seriously injured tonight."

"I know. The perp is escalating, getting bolder," Stone commented. "He'll make a mistake and we'll catch him."

Riggs gritted his teeth. But would they catch him before Kate got hurt?

KATE HAD BEEN in shock over her car exploding and irritated at the graffiti, but she was furious someone had had the audacity to attack her at home.

Everything Kate had worked for the last few years had been to honor the town and her mother and the ones who'd died in the shooting. She'd dreamed of nothing more than bringing Briar Ridge back to glory with happy kids, adults, families and tourists, and to diminish the distrust riddling the town.

But someone so opposed to those things was willing to kill her.

"Kate," Stone said in a quiet tone. "Did anyone approach you at the picnic? Someone you perceived as a threat?"

"Just Billy." The scene between Macy and Trey flashed behind her eyes. Then Brynn with Gretta. Altercations that had nothing to do with her. Had they?

The scene between Macy and Trey especially bothered Kate. It hinted at domestic violence. Although, Macy was helping to investigate the shooting. Perhaps she'd uncovered something and had confronted Trey about it.

At one time, Kate would have known. Macy would have shared her fears and details about her relationship. Although she had been withdrawn at times. Hadn't talked about her mother's illness.

Maybe something had happened that Kate didn't know about. What if Macy had trouble in her marriage and needed Kate? Perhaps she was the one who'd let down her friend. She should have reached out.

"I'm going to issue an APB for Billy Hodgkins. It's time he answered some questions." Stone stepped aside to make the call, and Riggs rubbed Kate's shoulder.

"Did you see Don Gaines hanging around anywhere?" Riggs asked.

Kate searched her memory banks. "No. I noticed Gretta arguing with Brynn at the picnic. I don't know what they were talking about, though, but Gretta wouldn't leave Brynn alone."

Riggs shrugged. "I know. Jay ran to her rescue. He always despised Gretta."

He wasn't the only one.

"Gretta stopped by the school the day you found

that graffiti. Maybe she was fishing for the reason Don was there."

Kate shifted. "Or maybe Gretta knows something about all this that we don't."

"That could be true," Riggs said. "She sure as hell seems to be in everyone's business just like she was back in the day."

Kate shuddered.

"I want to look at that pipe bomb," Riggs said. "Meanwhile, think, Kate. Did you see anything else that seemed suspicious at the picnic?"

"Nothing about the school, but Trey and Macy were arguing. He got rough with her and grabbed her arm. I told him to back off."

"How did he react?" Riggs asked.

Kate shivered. "He got mad and told me to mind my own business."

Riggs cleared his throat. "Did you hear what they were arguing about?"

"No, and Macy told me she could handle it," Kate said. "But the look in his eyes...it bordered on abusive."

"Macy is FBI," Riggs pointed out. "She seems tough, not the type to be victimized."

Yet Kate knew Macy's secrets. "Even strong women get caught off guard by the men they love," Kate said softly. Especially a seasoned manipulator.

Pain wrenched Riggs's face and Kate realized she'd hit a nerve. She'd forgotten about the gossip that Riggs's father had been abusive to his mother. "I'm sorry, Riggs, I didn't mean to be insensitive."

A muscle ticked in his jaw. "No problem. If Trey deserves it, I'm sure Macy will kick him to the curb, too."

She hoped so. Although, deep down, Macy had insecurities caused by her mother's mental health issues. A vulnerable spot that an abuser might prey on.

Surely her FBI training would have taught her how to overcome being a victim.

Riggs's brow creased. "Trey's father was a hunter, wasn't he? And Trey used to go with him."

"I did hear that," Kate admitted. "His father owned a gun shop outside town."

"Right," Riggs said thoughtfully. "Trey liked to brag about his father's gun collection." Riggs heaved a breath. "Dammit. What if Trey sold Ned that gun he used to commit the shooting?"

Kate paled. "If he did, maybe Macy figured it out and that's why they were arguing."

RIGGS LOWERED HIS VOICE. "We can't jump to conclusions, but it's worth asking Stone about. Macy could have seen something in the old files that aroused her suspicions."

Kate rubbed her fingers together in that nervous gesture he'd come to recognize. "Now I'm really worried about her."

"Don't, Kate. Macy can take care of herself."

She didn't look convinced. "I'm going to talk to Stone," Riggs said.

While he hurried up to the house, Riggs struggled to remember if he'd ever seen Trey talking to Ned in high school. Trey had been cocky and had always had a chip on his shoulder. He'd driven a motorcycle, was on the wrestling team, and possessed a dark, bad boy side that attracted girls.

Trey would never have been friendly with Ned. But Trey's family had guns and Trey was a loose cannon.

A possible scenario played through his mind. Trey could have met up with Ned some place where no one would have seen them. Some place he could have given, or sold, him a gun.

And after the shooting, Trey had kept quiet because he'd realized he was complicit in multiple murders.

The smoke was clearing slightly inside the house, although debris from the pipe bomb littered the wood floor and a charred odor permeated the space.

Brian gestured across the room. "We managed to keep it from spreading to the bedrooms."

That was good, although there would be water and smoke damage.

"I want to look at the bomb," Riggs said.

"Just don't touch anything," Stone said. "There may be prints somewhere in there."

"It's not my first crime scene," Riggs said, annoyed at the reminder.

"Sorry," Stone said. "Habit."

Riggs gave a nod then relayed his conversation with Kate.

"Did Kate hear what Trey and Macy were arguing about?" Stone asked.

Riggs shook his head no. "But Kate said it looked like Trey was getting physical with Macy."

A dark look crossed Stone's face. "I'll talk to her. Maybe she has insight into Trey and the gun."

Riggs thanked him and crossed the room. Shattered glass crunched beneath his boots as he snapped pictures of the debris on the floor and the damage the pipe bomb had caused. Once he had his pictures, Riggs tugged on latex gloves and squatted to examine the bomb materials.

"You say it was thrown through the sliders?" Brian asked.

"Yeah." Riggs pointed to the floor. "It landed here."

Brian squatted beside him, and Riggs noticed a photo of Kate and her mother that had been shattered in the explosion. Her father wasn't present in any of the pictures, reminding him that she'd never mentioned him. He wondered what the story was there.

In the photograph, Kate looked to be about ten and was wearing a pair of small wire-rimmed glasses. She was young and innocent, and held a book in her hand.

He smiled at the image. The bookshelf by her fireplace overflowed with paperbacks—romance, mystery, family stories.

But his smile faded as he turned back to examine the crime scene.

"Looks amateurish," Riggs said. "Whoever did this used match heads and gun powder."

"I agree. Anyone, even a kid, could make one of these," Brian noted. "All you need is the internet."

"And some basic materials you could pick up anywhere," Riggs mumbled.

Stone joined them, his hands on his hips. "My deputy found Billy and is bringing him in. Once the crime team arrives, I'll question him. What are your thoughts on the bomb, Riggs?"

Riggs gestured toward the pipe. "Not sophisticated at all. I know Billy is a suspect, but the amateurish aspects of the bomb and graffiti suggest we might be looking at a teenager." He pointed to the pipe. "This is an exhaust pipe from a car."

"Or someone who doesn't know what they're doing. The bomber could have gotten the pipe at a car repair shop," Stone said.

"Or a junkyard," Riggs added with a shrug.

"Maybe Billy was just desperate," Brian suggested "and he didn't have time to put together something more sophisticated."

Stone scratched his head. "Don Gaines was in the science lab that day someone painted the threat on the wall."

Riggs sucked in a breath. "Yeah, but I still don't understand his motive."

Stone shrugged. "Maybe he just has anger issues. I'll follow up on the fingerprints. If his match the ones on the matchbook we found in his locker, I'll bring him in."

"Have the team see if they can lift prints from the piping material," Riggs said.

If they did, and the prints matched Billy's or Don's, they'd nail the culprit before he hurt anyone.

THE HOUSE WAS going to be damaged. Kate made a mental list to call her insurance company and her general contractor to get an estimate for repairs.

Finally the firemen emerged and began to pack up

to leave. Riggs came out a minute later with Stone, his face grim.

"How bad is it?" she asked.

"Not too bad," Riggs said. "Some smoke and water damage, but it was contained to the living room area." He gave her a sympathetic smile. "I'm sorry, Kate."

Kate shrugged. "It's only things," she said. After losing her mother, she could survive anything except losing someone else she loved.

"You can't stay here tonight, Kate," Riggs said. "Go pack an overnight bag and you can arrange for a clean-up crew in the morning."

She wanted to argue, be brave. Insist that she wouldn't let anyone scare her away from her own home.

But as she climbed the porch steps and reached the door, the acrid odor of the explosive hit her. And was a reminder that someone was stalking her.

She'd survived tonight. What if he succeeded the next time?

Stepping into the foyer, Kate's stomach clenched at the mess in her house. Water soaked the wood floor and furniture, and smoke stained the walls and flooring. The kitchen had survived, but the walls would probably need a fresh coat of paint, as well.

Her briefcase holding the plans for the memorial sat on the table by the door, thankfully undamaged. The pictures of her and her mother on the mantel were safe. And so was she. That was all that mattered.

"Careful where you walk," Riggs said. "And don't touch anything in the living room. The crime team needs to process the room for evidence."

"Understood."

She carefully picked her way along the wall to the bedroom. Inside the closet, she retrieved her overnight bag, tossed her toiletries, pajamas and a dress for the dedication ceremony inside, then slipped back through the living room.

Riggs was waiting by the door, a scowl deepening his face. Outside, voices indicated the crime investigators had arrived. She snagged her briefcase and purse, and Riggs took her overnight bag as they stepped through the door.

Stone directed the crime team toward the porch just as she and Riggs reached her rental SUV.

"I'll have them lock up when they're finished," Stone said.

Kate thanked him. "I'll call my contractor and insurance company in the morning."

Riggs opened the rear door and set her bag inside. "Follow me to my house, Kate."

She shrugged. "Thanks, but I'll stay at the inn."

Rigg's jaw hardened. "You'll be safer at my place."

Not when she wanted to crawl into his arms. "I'll be fine at the inn. Most of the alumni are staying there."

Her stomach knotted. There might not be room though, but she had to try. Although one of the guests could be her enemy.

Chapter Sixteen

In spite of Kate's protests, Riggs insisted on following her to the inn to make sure she got settled safely, then walked her inside.

She admired the changes Celeste, the owner, had made on the exterior before she went inside. Last year, when Kate had first broached the local business owners and town council with the idea of inviting all former alumni to the dedication ceremony and combining it with a class reunion, Celeste had jumped on the idea of a renovation to the inn.

Celeste had lived in Briar Ridge for over twenty-five years. She remembered the glory days of sipping sweet iced tea on the porch with neighbors, when locking the doors to your house and car were things other people did, not the friendly trustworthy residents of the small town who loved one another and welcomed strangers into its fold with open arms.

The town had embraced Elaine McKendrick as a single mother. Half the ladies in town had babysat for Kate at some time before she reached school age. The local church had put on fundraisers for needy families, organized Habitat for Humanity projects and each year hosted a charity Christmas party for the hospital.

When Kate was in elementary school, she had helped her mother decorate and read to the sick children, after which they'd passed out cookies, hot chocolate and presents.

Celeste had allowed families to stay at the inn, either free or at a discount rate, while their children underwent medical treatment.

She'd given the same loving care to restoring the inn by replacing rotting boards, painting the two-story country farmhouse a pale yellow, and adding flowerbeds and crepe myrtles which made the place postcard-pretty. New rocking chairs and porch swings added homey touches to the wraparound porch, and a gazebo and seating areas in the garden gave it even more charm. Purple, pink and white petunias filled one section while sunflowers danced in the breeze in another. She'd even stocked the small pond behind the gardens for guests who wanted to fish.

Judging from the parking lot, the inn was bustling tonight. Still shaken by the pipe bomb, Kate headed to the front desk and greeted Celeste.

"The inn looks beautiful," Kate said. "The rosebushes in front are gorgeous."

Celeste blushed. "I had to have roses," she said. "The garden has several different varieties."

"You've done a wonderful job," Kate said, remembering how much her mother loved roses. "But tonight I had a fire at my house and I'm looking for a room."

"Oh, my gosh." Celeste glanced at Riggs, then back at Kate. "Are you all right, dear?"

Kate faked a smile. How could she be all right when someone wanted her dead? "It was scary, but I'm okay now."

Celeste tapped a pen on the guest registry. "I'm sorry, hon, but I don't have any rooms available this week. The reunion drew so many alumni to town that we're completely booked."

Kate should have expected as much. But what was she going to do? She couldn't go home…"Thanks. I'm glad you're busy and hope you will be from now on."

Celeste fanned her face. "My nephew is so smart, he made a website and posted pictures on Facebook. He even ran Facebook ads, and we're asking folks who stay here to leave online reviews. So far, I have two more weeks filled this month."

"I'm really happy," Kate said. "I hope this week gives you the business boost you need."

The older woman squeezed Kate's hand. "I'm proud of what you're doing," Celeste said. "Shame on those folks at the meeting for giving you a hard time."

Kate thanked her again then stepped away and glanced at Riggs. Her stomach twisted.

"The offer still stands, Kate," Riggs said. "Just follow me to my place. You'll be safe there."

She sighed but didn't have a choice so she nodded.

Woody Mathis staggered through the door, spotted Kate and snarled something ugly beneath his breath. Riggs started toward him, but Kate clutched his arm and moved aside to avoid him. Orson Johnson, who'd lost his arm from the elbow down in the shooting, followed Woody in. Orson was balding, his face pudgy, his expression bitter. In high school, he'd played football, but his family had moved away after the shooting. She'd heard he raised chickens in North Georgia somewhere.

But she hadn't seen him in years. "Hi, Orson," she said. "Welcome back to town."

He shot her a look of resentment. "Only reason I came is to see that damned old building torn down."

"Then you're in favor of the new school?" Kate asked.

Orson shoved his Falcons hat up on his head. "Sure am."

Woody jerked his thumb at Kate. "She ought to be telling everyone how sorry she is," Woody said, his words overlapping. "She's the reason Ned pulled the trigger."

Riggs eased Kate behind him. "Kate is not any more responsible than the rest of us who ignored or teased Ned. I don't recall you being friends with him, Woody."

Woody staggered sideways, his shoulder bumping the wall. "Hell, he wasn't in love with me…"

"There was more to Ned's problems than Kate rejecting him for a date," Riggs snapped. "And, I thought you were in jail."

"Bail," Woody said, slurring the word. "Can't keep a man locked up for something he didn't do."

"You shot at Stone," Riggs pointed out.

Woody chuckled. "That was an accident. My finger slipped."

Kate shifted and wrapped her arms around her waist.

"Come on, Kate, let's go." He tugged on Kate's arm, coaxing her toward the exit.

"That's it, run and hide behind Riggs," Woody taunted.

Kate wanted to scream at him that she wasn't doing that. Except she *was*.

"Go sleep it off," Riggs growled.

Kate pushed open the door and stepped into the fresh air, her lungs straining.

Woody cursed as he gripped the rail to go upstairs, and Orson followed, mumbling something about wishing the whole damn town would burn down.

Riggs heaved a sigh as he joined Kate on the front stoop of the inn. "Woody is a jerk, but he's all mouth and stays drunk most of the time. I don't think he's got the guts to make a bomb and throw it in your house."

"He needs AA," Kate said.

"Yeah, or to be locked up for his own good."

"I didn't realize Orson was so bitter," Kate said, unsettled by his comments.

"Sounds like Woody's been feeding his anger. And that comment about him wanting the town to burn down makes me wonder." Riggs scrubbed a hand through his thick hair. "I'll call Stone once we get to my place, tell him what Woody said and ask him to look into Orson."

They hurried down the steps, and Kate veered toward her vehicle while Riggs climbed into his truck.

A gust of wind whipped through the trees, thunder rumbling. Just as Kate unlocked the door, a car door opened and slammed shut. Nerves on edge, she glanced up to see Trey vault from a black Range Rover and stalk toward her. His broad body was just as intimidating as his sinister expression.

"Trey." Kate gripped her keys in a self-defense move.

Trey curled both beefy hands on her shoulders and squeezed hard. Then he pushed his face into hers, nostrils flared. "What happens between me and my wife is our business, Kate. You may think you own this town, but you'll never tell me what to do, so stay away from me and Macy."

RAGE HEATED RIGGS's blood at the sight of Trey's hands on Kate. He jumped from his truck, crossed the distance in two strides, and yanked Trey away from her.

"Take your hands off of her," Riggs stormed.

Anger radiated from Trey in palpable waves. "I'll do what I damn well please, Benford."

"The hell you will," Riggs growled. "Touch her again, and you'll pay for it."

Trey barked a nasty sound. "Right. Like you're going to beat me up?"

"At least I know how to treat a woman," Riggs snapped. "Kate and your wife both deserve respect, not to be manhandled."

"You don't know anything about my wife or me." Trey shoved Riggs backward.

Riggs started to retaliate, but Kate grabbed his arm. "Don't," Kate said softly. "You're not like him, Riggs."

Maybe he wasn't. But he sure as hell didn't intend to let the jerk hurt Kate.

"Let's just go," Kate said. "He's not worth it."

Riggs ushered Kate into her SUV. "Start the engine and drive out of the parking lot. I'm right behind you."

"Riggs, please," Kate said.

He squeezed her hand gently. "Go. I'll follow you."

Trey's boots crunched gravel as he stepped toward Riggs.

Riggs held up a warning hand. "I don't want to fight with you, Trey. This town has seen enough trouble. Just stay away from Kate."

Trey heaved a breath. Every muscle in the man's body was wound tight with the urge to fight, as if he was barely holding on to his rage.

Riggs didn't give him time to make a move. He strode to his truck, got in and cranked the engine, keeping his eyes on Trey the entire time. As he drove from the parking lot, he checked his rearview mirror to make sure the bastard hadn't pulled a gun or followed him.

He caught up with Kate as she turned onto the road. Using his hands-free app, he called Stone. When Stone's voice mail responded, Riggs left a message relaying what had happened with Trey, Woody and Orson.

Remembering Kate had never been to his place, he maneuvered around her so she could follow him.

He wanted her safe at home with him tonight.

KATE COULDN'T SHAKE Orson's comments as she followed Riggs around the curvy road. How in the world had she made so many enemies?

She'd hoped the reunion would bring people together. Instead, her plan seemed to be backfiring.

Riggs veered onto a side road leading to a cluster

of cabins offering privacy and views of the river and mountains. She parked in the graveled drive behind him, a frisson of nerves dancing along her spine.

She'd never been to his house and coming here tonight seemed…intimate. Made her wish for a real friendship with Riggs. Or more.

Shutting out the foolish thought, she climbed from her vehicle. A summer storm breeze stirred the air, bringing the aromas of honeysuckle and pine, heavenly scents that reminded her why she liked living in the area. Though she enjoyed vacations at the beach, the stunning peaks and ridges of the Blue Ridge Mountains and closeness to nature filled her with a sense of peace and tranquility. This was home.

Although tonight those mountains looked dark and ominous, a reminder that the rolling hills and dense forests offered dozens of places for the person after her to hide.

Stomach knotted with anxiety, she retrieved her purse, overnight bag and briefcase from the back seat. A second later, Riggs grabbed the overnight bag from her and carried it to the house. She'd never been to Riggs's place, having expected him to have a bachelor pad in town. But this rustic cabin with its stunning mountain view looked cozy and welcoming. The sound of the river behind his cabin was musical and reminded her of swimming in the summer as a kid. She imagined Riggs fishing out back or canoeing on a Sunday. The front porch held two rockers that called her name, but she was so exhausted, she bypassed them and followed Riggs inside instead.

As they entered, moonlight glittered off Riggs's dark hair and glowed through the massive windows overlooking the river. The nine-foot ceilings made the open-concept living room and kitchen seem large and airy. A stacked stone fireplace climbed the wall to the ceiling, flanked by built-in bookcases in a rich dark wood. The kitchen cabinets matched, contrasted by white quartz counters. A peninsula added bar seating, the base of the stools made of tree trunks, the seats, a rich brown leather.

The dark leather couch, painting of wild Mustangs, and plaid club chair gave the room a masculine feel. Yet there was something missing here. No personal touches, no family pictures. "It's beautiful," she said.

A sheepish look crossed Riggs's face. "Thanks. I built here for the view, and the seclusion."

"I like the furnishings, and the view is breathtaking," Kate said, although the way the moonlight through window framed Riggs's tall, muscular body was just as breathtaking as the outdoor scenery.

"There are two bedrooms." Riggs gestured toward the right. "A private bath is attached to the guest room. Make yourself at home."

Kate admired the rustic shiplap as he set her bag on the bed. A blue and white quilt in a Dresden pattern adorned the four-poster bed.

She traced her fingers over the intricate pattern. "This is stunning, Riggs. Did your mother make it?"

"She did," he said, a smile lighting his face. "I used to watch her quilt in front of the fireplace at night."

"I saw some of her quilts at the festivals," Kate said.

"She was an excellent seamstress and really creative in her designs."

"I hear quilting is a lost art," Riggs said. "But they were popular with tourists back in the day, and she made enough for us to get by."

That was the most personal thing he'd shared. "I think they'd still be popular if we had tourists coming in." Kate blinked back tears. "I'd like to see the town lively like that again."

Riggs grunted in agreement and then an awkward silence fell between them for a minute and they returned to the living room. Finally, Kate spoke. "Thank you for letting me spend the night."

Riggs walked toward her, a protective gleam in his eyes. "There's no way I'd let you stay alone, not after what happened today."

A shudder coursed up Kate's spine. "The dedication ceremony is tomorrow," Kate said. "Once the publicity dies down, maybe whoever's threatening me will give up and leave town." At least, she prayed that would happen.

"Maybe. But if it's Ned's accomplice, he needs to pay for all the lives he destroyed."

"That's true." Kate rubbed her arms with her hands, noticing the single picture on the bookshelf above the corner desk. A photograph of firefighters in uniform. "Did you become a firefighter because of the shooting?"

Riggs clenched his jaw. "Yeah. Took me a while to get my act together, though," he said, rubbing at his thigh where the bullet had struck him. "I was bitter at first. Angry. I hated being disabled."

Kate swallowed hard. "You lost your scholarship."

He nodded. "That wasn't the worst part, though. For a while, I thought I might not ever be useful."

"Oh, Riggs, I'm so sorry."

"It wasn't your fault, Kate. My injury was nothing compared to what some others went through. At least I survived." He heaved a weary breath. "I even felt guilty about that."

"I know what you mean." Emotions clogged Kate's throat. "But you still had reason to be bitter. Instead, you turned your life around and made something of yourself."

He shrugged as if he didn't deserve her praise. "I hated being helpless that day. I saw you running to help others, and wanted to do the same, but I couldn't get up."

"It was chaotic and I was terrified," Kate admitted. "I didn't want to leave Mom, but she told me to go, to help the others."

An understanding smile crossed Riggs's face. "That sounds like her."

Kate's heart warmed and some of her earlier tension melted away.

"Why a firefighter?" she finally asked.

Riggs cleared his throat. "Because the first responders rushed inside the school that day and were heroes," he said. "Later, once I got past the self-pity, I realized I wanted to be like them. That I never wanted to be helpless again. That's when I got serious about PT."

Kate's heart squeezed. Like many of their classmates, Riggs would be featured on the memorial wall she had planned for the new school. No one would forget that tragedy, but out of it, unsung heroes had been born.

She hoped their stories and the wall would inspire other students to overcome adversity. Amy had collected information on individual students for months to help with the project.

Kate pressed a hand over Riggs's. "The last thing my mother said before she died was for me to make something good come of the shooting that day. It's taken me years to figure out how to do that."

Riggs's eyes darkened. "And you are. You're amazing, Kate."

"So are you, Riggs."

Riggs's breath quickened and he traced a finger along her jaw. The gentle gesture was so erotic and comforting that Kate couldn't resist.

She wanted to forget about today, about the fire and danger, about the town and the reunion. She wanted to forget that her two best friends were no longer speaking to her and she didn't know how to mend their friendships.

Suddenly needy, she licked her suddenly dry lips and stood on tiptoe.

His mouth parted, his chest rose and fell unevenly, and he angled his head toward hers.

Kate closed her eyes and pressed her lips over Riggs's. Need spiraled through her. For the last few days, Riggs had been a pillar of strength.

She didn't want to be afraid anymore.

She wanted his touch, his kiss, his hands on her.

RIGGS ORDERED HIMSELF not to rush Kate, but when her lips met his, rational thought died a sudden death.

Kate tasted like the most potent combination of sweetness and spice. Heat coursed through his blood, need and desire splintered his control, and he pulled her against his body and deepened the kiss. She moaned softly, an invitation for more, and he teased her lips apart with his tongue then dove inside to explore.

She threaded her fingers through his hair and drew him closer. Her breasts pressed against the hard planes of his chest and drove him mad with want.

Being with Kate meant more than a night of sex. He liked Kate. Cared about her.

He hesitated a moment at that thought then realized he'd never allowed anyone to get close to him. Losing friends and his mother had taught him to protect his heart.

Kate whispered his name and ran her hands over his back, stroking his muscles, and he forgot about protecting himself. He dipped his head and planted kisses along her neck and throat. She moaned softly and tilted her head back, offering him access to the succulent skin between her breasts.

He itched to strip her clothes and take her right there. On the floor. In the doorway. On the couch. Anywhere she'd have him.

No… Kate deserved better.

She clung to him, and he walked them backward to the guest bed, wrapping one arm around her waist while he cupped her breast with his other hand. She felt full and heavy, her nipple puckering against the silk of her blouse.

His body hardened.

He whispered her name then eased the buttons of her blouse apart, this time revealing a thin, lacy black bra that barely contained her plump breasts. They were ripe now, begging for attention.

Riggs teased one nipple with his teeth while he raked his thumb over the other. She sighed again, breathy and needy, and raked her foot up his calf.

Her low moan of pleasure heated his blood, and he thought he might explode. But giving Kate pleasure overrode his need.

He tugged the lace aside, exposing her skin, and sucked in a sharp breath as passion exploded inside him. Kate moaned, and he closed his lips around one turgid peak and tugged it in his mouth. Cupping her rear with his other hand, he suckled her, deep and long, hard and hungrily, before he moved to the other breast and gave it the same loving attention.

"Riggs," Kate whispered.

Her raspy voice made him pause, and he looked up to see her eyes glazed with passion. But something else lurked in the depths of her eyes—fear?

Pulse pounding, he gently tilted her chin up and forced her to look at him. "Kate, do you want me to stop?"

Chapter Seventeen

Stopping made perfect sense. It was the logical, smart thing to do. Keep her distance. Stand on her own.

Except logic floated out the window as Kate searched Riggs's gaze for any sign he was simply using her for sex. Instead, passion and sincerity shone in his smoky eyes.

His protective nature touched her deeply. She'd been alone so long that she'd forgotten what it felt like to have someone care about her.

"Kate?" Riggs's breath rasped out, making him sound almost...vulnerable. Slowly, he lowered his hands from her shoulders. "I understand."

The tenderness in his tone and his willingness to walk away intensified her desire. Ever since she'd lost her mother, she'd been terrified of giving her heart to anyone.

But Riggs already owned it.

She was tired of being afraid. Of running from what she wanted.

Kate caught his arm, her heart on her sleeve. "Don't leave. I...want you, Riggs."

Her heart fluttered at the way his eyes softened when he smiled at her. With a throaty groan, he yanked her into his arms again and claimed her mouth with his. Kate succumbed to the heat burning between them and tugged at his shirt. Seconds later, he pulled it over his head and tossed it to the floor. The sight of his broad chest dusted in a soft mat of dark hair intensified her desire, and she raked her hands over his chest.

Riggs unbuttoned the remaining buttons on her blouse and gently peeled the fabric away. Cool air met her bare skin, yet she felt as if she was on fire.

She slipped her arms out of the sleeves and her shirt hit the floor beside his. His eyes narrowed, raking over her in a hungry look, then he eased her back onto the bed.

Seconds later, clothes flew off and hands and lips touched and teased, evoking erotic sensations that spiraled out of control.

Riggs trailed his lips across her naked breasts, sucking her nipples until liquid heat pooled between her thighs. She arched her back, moaning his name as he licked his way down her stomach, then he pushed her legs apart and dove into her damp heat with his tongue.

Her body quivered with sensations, need building as waves of pleasure rippled through her. He teased and tormented her with his tongue, then lifted her hips to allow him access as he made love to her with his mouth. One flick of his tongue across her sweet spot, then another and another, and she cried out his name as her orgasm rocked through her.

RIGGS'S BLOOD BURNED hot as Kate threw her head back in ecstasy.

He'd given her that pleasure. He didn't want it to end.

He kissed her again, letting her taste her own sweet release, then snatched a condom from his jeans and rolled it on. Kate watched, her eyes darkening, her chest rising and falling erratically. Her breasts begged for attention again, and he stroked her inner thighs as he twisted her nipples between his fingers. She arched into him, gripped his shoulders and whispered his name on a throaty moan, the pull between them growing more intense.

Her excitement magnified his own, and he slipped a finger inside her heat as he tugged one of her nipples between his teeth and suckled her again. Her slick wet chamber clenched around his finger and he added another one, teasing her as he stroked her body.

"Riggs, please," she whispered. "I want you inside me."

She didn't have to ask twice. He wanted to make her his, completely.

He kneed her legs further apart, then sank his hard length inside her with a groan. She gasped for a breath, and he pulled out then thrust into her again, penetrating her. Blinded by need, he repeated the motion, building a rhythm charged with raw desire. She gripped his hips and guided him deeper, their bodies gliding together, the friction building to a crescendo.

Sweat beaded on his skin as he thrust into her again and again. She dug her nails into his back, clinging to him as he rode her hard and fast.

Seconds later, Kate moaned his name as another orgasm splintered through her. He wanted to join her.

Holding her as the sensations built, Riggs gripped her hips, driving himself deeper, over and over, until their bodies shook with pleasure.

One deep thrust, then he pulled out and thrust again, lifting her hips so he could fill her deeper. She raked her nails down his back, the depth of her passion sending him over the edge. His release hit him, hot and mind-numbing.

And sweet. Even sweeter because he knew Kate didn't give herself to any man easily.

Quickly disposing of the condom, he rolled Kate to her side and cradled her in his arms until she fell asleep, sated and curled against him.

KATE WOKE TO the sound of Riggs's soft snoring. For a moment, she lay still, savoring the moment. His big body was so warm and strong that she felt safe and loved in a way she hadn't felt before.

He'd treated her to a pleasure she'd never experienced because his lovemaking had been giving. Her breasts tingled just at the thought of his lips suckling her.

But sunshine poured through the window, a reminder today was the culmination of months of work and planning. The dedication ceremony was scheduled for two o'clock. She needed to make sure everything was on track.

Amy planned to meet her at the site early so they could set up the memorial display together.

Riggs stirred, rolled over and opened his eyes. A smile tilted the corner of his sexy mouth, tempting her to stay in bed and make love to him again.

But today was too important to be late.

"Morning," Riggs murmured.

Kate's heart fluttered. She imagined what it would be like to wake up every day beside this incredible man, and realized she was falling for Riggs.

"I need to shower. I'm meeting Amy at the site," Kate said. "We have to set things up for the ceremony this afternoon."

He drew her to him for a long, slow kiss, and temptation almost won.

But the image of Cassidy and her son Roy taunted her, and Kate scanned the room for her shirt or something to cover up with when she got out of bed.

Riggs ran a hand over her bare hip. "You're beautiful, Kate. You don't have to hide that body from me."

How had he read her mind?

A blush climbed her neck and she inhaled. "I need to get ready."

"And I need to make love to you again," Riggs said in a low whisper.

Kate stilled, her pulse clamoring as he cupped her breasts in his hands. "Riggs…"

"Yeah, it's me, Kate. Remember how it feels for me to be inside you." He pushed his thick length between her buttocks and stroked her, and pleasure shot through her.

One last time. She just needed him one more time then she could walk away and he could go to Cassidy or his next lover.

That thought hurt, but she banished it as her breasts throbbed beneath his fingers. He seemed to read her mind again, turned her around, lowered his head and tugged one peak into his mouth. Then he trailed his fingers down to her heat. He sucked the other turgid peak while his fingers claimed her, and she clawed at his back as erotic sensations pummeled her.

On the brink of an orgasm, he snagged a condom, rolled it on, rose above her and entered her with one swift thrust. Kate clung to him, parting her legs so he could dive deeper. He groaned, lifted her and she wrapped her legs around his waist as he pumped inside her.

His hips thrust forward, his hard length sinking so deep inside she felt him to the core. A second later, release splintered through her as if a match had been lit inside her and erupted into flames. Riggs captured her groan with his mouth as he kissed her, then he joined her on the ride as he came inside her.

Perspiration beaded Riggs's skin as he held Kate in his arms. When she'd first started to slip from bed, he told himself to let her. But then she'd blushed and looked shy, and he wanted Kate to know how much he wanted her. How much he liked her body.

Hell, he liked everything about Kate.

He trailed a hand over her hip as their orgasms slowly subsided and leaned his head against hers. "Kate—"

"Shh, you don't have to say anything." Kate eased from his arms. "I know how this works."

He tensed at her tone. He disposed of the condom then turned back to her. "What do you mean?"

Kate folded her arms in front of her breasts as if she could hide the glorious mounds. But the image and feel of them were imprinted in his brain forever.

"I mean I have to go." She licked her lips. "And when this situation is cleared up, I won't expect anything."

There she was, treating him like a womanizer again. "I'm not sure I do."

Some emotion he couldn't identify flickered across her face. "I know you like being a bachelor."

"I like being with you," he said.

A tense heartbeat passed. "What about Cassidy?"

His eyes narrowed to slits. "What about her?"

"I saw you with her yesterday," Kate said. "And then there's her son."

Cold anger balled in his chest. "Yes, she has a son. But I'm not interested in Cassidy, Kate. I never have been."

Confusion clouded her eyes then something akin to anger. "But you have a child—"

He reached for his clothes and began yanking them on, his movements abrupt. "You're certain Cassidy's son is mine, aren't you?"

Kate rose and backed toward the bathroom. "That's what I heard and—"

"And you believe it," Riggs said in disgust. "I thought you were above taking gossip at face value, Kate."

She opened her mouth to speak, but he was too furious to listen. Or maybe he was just hurt. He thought he'd proved he was different than her high school image of him.

"Riggs—"

"Go shower, Kate. I'm going to do the same." Without another word, he strode to his room then to his bathroom and slammed the door. He stared at himself in the mirror, furious with himself for letting down his guard.

He was sated from the best lovemaking he'd ever had.

And disappointed that he wanted their lovemaking to mean more.

He'd never felt those emotions after sex before. Had always just walked away, no attachments, no entanglements. No hurt feelings on either side.

He flipped on the water, undressed, then climbed beneath the hot spray and scrubbed his body as if he was as dirty as Kate thought him to be.

But he couldn't scrub away the pain of her words.

Maybe you should have told her the truth.

Maybe.

But Kate had never asked. She'd just believed the worst of him. And that hurt more than anything.

KATE DREADED FACING Riggs after her shower. But she held her head high. Today was important—the day of the dedication ceremony. She had to focus and get through it.

Before she joined Riggs in the kitchen, she arranged for someone to clean up the mess made by the pipe bomb at her house. The repair crew, a local one she'd used before, assured her they'd have it finished by the afternoon. The painting would have to come later, but at least she could stay at home tonight.

Riggs remained silent and brooding as she poured herself a cup of coffee. He was already sipping a cup as he watched the local morning news on TV. First the weather, then a story about Briar Ridge.

"Folks, this is Gretta Wright with a breaking story," Gretta said with a smile. "I'm coming to you from the town of Briar Ridge, most known for the school shooting fifteen years ago. Despite protests from vocal locals, high school principal Kate McKendrick spearheaded efforts to demolish the old school building in light of a newer modern facility.

"But this week, while alumni have swarmed to town for a class reunion and the celebration for the new school, Kate McKendrick has come under fire. Literally. While driving home from a town meeting, her car burst into flames. Police have confirmed that the fire was no accident. Neither was the fire that was set behind Ms. McKendrick's property. Threats to her also include graffiti on the high school and a pipe bomb that was thrown into her house." She paused for emphasis. "An inside source also revealed that Ms. McKendrick received a threatening letter blaming her for the shooter massacring his classmates."

Kate gasped.

"My God, how did she find out about the letter?" Kate pressed a hand over her heart. "The only people I told were you and Stone."

Riggs's jaw hardened. "Good question."

Gretta's voice cut through her thoughts. "If you have

any information regarding these crimes or the attempts on Ms. McKendrick's life, please call the local police."

Frustrated, Kate flicked off the TV, poured her coffee in a to-go cup and grabbed her things.

Riggs followed, the silence stretching painfully between them as they went to their separate vehicles.

The reminder of the threat made Kate scan the area as she pulled from the driveway and drove to the building site to meet Amy. Amy hadn't arrived yet, so Kate parked near the construction trailer.

Workers were already inside, probably discussing the plans.

Riggs didn't get out of his pickup. Instead he drove away, a sign he was upset.

It was better this way. Better to stop the insanity before she completely fell in love with the man and he broke her heart.

Heaven help her. She *had* judged him. But how could she not? He hadn't denied that Roy was his child. He hadn't acknowledged him, either. Just like her father had never acknowledged her.

Her mother had tried to smooth over the truth, but it sat there raw and ugly every day of Kate's life. He hadn't wanted her. She'd been a mistake. He couldn't be saddled with a kid. He'd had places to go and things to do and that did not involve a sniveling, needy kid.

Maybe if she'd been a boy, a *son*, he might have loved her. Or maybe not. Maybe he was just weak and selfish and…and why did she care anyway? Why had she spent every birthday and Christmas wishing he'd show up and tell her he'd been wrong, that he really loved her.

Just like Riggs would leave one day. If her own father hadn't loved her, how could Riggs?

Roy Fulton probably felt the same way. He was a loner, had no friends. Kept his head in his computer and on his phone. Seemed sullen and angry. Maybe because he was fatherless, too.

What she didn't understand was that Riggs seemed changed. That he was a good man. He even volunteered at the kids' hospital. It didn't make sense.

While she waited on Amy, she checked her notes on her phone for details she needed to iron out. Basically everything was set, though.

The mayor should show up at one thirty along with the town council.

A sedan swerved into the parking lot and Amy emerged, her arms laden with a box of photos for the memorial. Grateful not to be alone, Kate hopped from her car and greeted her, although she kept her eyes peeled in case anyone else was lurking around.

Riggs had promised to protect her, yet he'd left her alone. That spoke volumes about how much he cared.

RIGGS SHOULDN'T HAVE left Kate alone. But he needed some time away from her, needed to put distance between them and regain control of his emotions. Kate made him think crazy things about the future.

Things he couldn't have. Like her. And a family.

She would be safe, he assured himself. The building crew was on site, and Amy was supposed to meet her any minute.

Dammit, how had Gretta learned about the letter Kate received?

Did she know who'd sent it? Or had Gretta sent the letter to stir up suspicion and interest for a big story?

Kate's comment about Cassidy's son still bothered him, too. She thought he was a deadbeat dad. A man who'd abandoned his child.

After the way his own old man had disappointed him, he'd vowed never to have kids. And if he had one, he'd do his best to be the kind of father he'd wanted.

For some reason, it was important that Kate believe in him. Trust him. Be the man she deserved. That meant owning up to the truth.

If he knew who Roy's father was, maybe he could convince Kate he was a stand-up guy.

He had to confront Cassidy. After all this time, he needed her to tell him once and for all who'd fathered her baby.

Determined to get to the truth, he sped toward Cassidy's. He had no idea if she'd show up at the celebration today, but she worked at the Cut and Dye, so he went there first.

Several cars were in the lot, more than usual, which made him curious if alumni were primping for tonight's dance. He pulled into a spot and parked, glancing around as he walked up to the entryway.

As he entered, hair dryers buzzed and the scent of hair products in the air hit him, almost smothering. There were four stations, each occupied with a client. Two were white-haired ladies while the other two clients looked to be about his age. He didn't recognize them. More alumni.

All eyes turned his way, whispers and voices echoing around him. Cassidy looked up and shot him a scowl when he motioned that he needed to talk to her. She spoke to her client then hurried over to him and gestured for him to step outside.

Once on the sidewalk, she jammed her hands on her hips, irritated. "What do you want, Riggs?"

"I want to know who Roy's father is," he said bluntly.

Cassidy narrowed her eyes into a scowl. "Why the hell are you asking me this *now*?"

"Because everyone in town thinks I'm his father and that I abandoned him, and I want it to stop."

Surprise flared in her eyes followed by a wariness that seeped through her lips as she pressed them into a tight line. "It's been years, Riggs. No one cares anymore."

"I care," he said. And Kate did. "What did you tell Roy?"

"My son and I are none of your business," she said.

"It's my business if Roy thinks I'm his father and I won't acknowledge him."

She heaved a breath then pushed her dyed-blond hair away from one cheek where the wind had tossed it. "He doesn't even know about you," she said. "Did it ever occur to you that I kept his father's name quiet to protect my son?"

She didn't wait for a response. She turned and stormed back into the salon, leaving Riggs to wonder what exactly she meant.

Why would Roy need protection from his father?

Kate and Amy spent the next two hours setting up the display. They showcased photographs on a tall blackboard to emulate how impressive it would look in the front hall of the new school.

The other part of the memorial was just as important. Amy had been working diligently for months collecting information on the students who'd survived and their accomplishments. One wall would feature photos with clippings of students who'd gained notoriety in some way, along with quotes and sayings from others about how the shooting had changed the trajectory of their lives.

Another board held copies of the sketch of the new sports fields and football stadium which they'd been promised would be ready by fall.

When she and Amy finished the display, they stood back to admire it. "I hope we have a good response to this," Kate said. "I want it to be inspirational for all the students at Briar Ridge High, past and present."

Amy squeezed Kate's shoulder. "I hope so, too, Kate. It's a wonderful way to honor the students and their loved ones." Amy glanced at her watch. "Hmm, I'm going to run over to the bakery to pick up the cupcakes for the celebration. I saw the news this morning, though. Will you be all right here?"

Kate nodded although, truthfully, nerves clawed at her. "I'm okay. The mayor should be here soon anyway, and the contractor is still at the construction trailer. Go pick up the cupcakes."

Amy looked reluctant to leave, but Kate checked the time and encouraged her to go.

Just as the dust settled from Amy's departure, the contractor exited the trailer, threw his hand up and waved, then jumped in his truck and peeled from the parking lot.

A gust of wind stirred, whistling through the trees as a dark cloud moved above, casting a shadow across the ground.

The hair on the back of Kate's neck prickled. Then the sound of footsteps crunching gravel echoed from behind her.

She swung around to see if another worker was in the trailer, but a cold voice stopped her.

"Don't make any sudden moves or I'll shoot you right here."

A second later, the cold barrel of a gun dug into her back.

HE JAMMED THE GUN into Kate McKendrick's back. He hadn't wanted it to come to this.

But Kate had pushed and pushed. Now everyone in town was talking about the shooting and asking questions about why Ned had done it and who might have helped him. He'd seen that nosy reporter's morning story about someone being after Kate.

She'd suggested the person who'd set the fire in the woods and tampered with Kate's car might be Ned's accomplice.

She had no idea how close she was. And how off base.

He hadn't been an accomplice.

He was part of the reason crazy Ned had turned that gun on the students at school.

Not that they hadn't deserved it. Some of them had.

There were others that hadn't been shot who were to blame, too.

Kate had dredged it all up.

And if that reporter kept poking her nose into everything, soon the truth would be exposed.

"Walk," he ordered as his hand gripped the gun.

He liked fire better than shooting. But he was desperate now and running out of time. He'd get rid of Kate any way he had to.

Then his secrets would be safe.

Chapter Eighteen

Riggs was still agitated when he met Stone at the police station. Macy was there, perched beside a whiteboard where Stone had posted pictures of persons of interest in the threats against Kate.

Another board held photos of the school shooting, along with pictures of the victims and photos with question marks beside them, noting them as possible accomplices.

"I saw Gretta on the news this morning," Stone said as he led him down the hall toward the interrogation rooms. "How's Kate?"

"Fine." But he was so *not* fine. Nope, not at all. "I left her at the new building site. She and Amy are preparing for the groundbreaking ceremony this afternoon.

"Do you know where Gretta got her information?" he asked Stone.

Stone shook his head. "Not a clue. I sure as hell didn't tell anyone about that letter of blame." He led Riggs to a room where he could view his interview with Billy via a computer monitor.

"Thanks, man. I appreciate you letting me observe."

Stone studied him for a minute. "Sure. But stay here. At no point are you allowed in the interrogation room. If he confesses, I want it to stick. And going all postal on him won't help."

Riggs gritted his teeth. "Do I look like I'd go postal?"

Stone smirked. "I don't know, but something's going on with you, and you're not thinking clearly."

Yeah, because a certain sexy woman was messing with his head.

He dropped into the chair in front of the monitor and raised his three fingers in a Boy Scout salute. Although he'd never been a Boy Scout. "Promise not to move."

Stone gave a wry laugh then closed the door. A minute later, he entered the interrogation room. Billy Hodgkins was fidgeting in his chair, toying with something between his fingers, although Riggs couldn't see what the object was.

"So, Billy…" Stone began. "Here we are."

Billy lifted his shoulders in a shrug. "Yeah, I just don't know why."

Stone claimed the chair opposite Billy, folded his arms and scrutinized Billy. "I think you do."

Billy worked his mouth from side to side. "If this is about Kate, I told you I just wanted to talk to her."

"And when she didn't want to talk to you, you got angry?"

Billy looked down at the table as if studying the scarred grooves in the wood.

"So you made a pipe bomb and tossed it into her house to either get her attention," Stone said matter-of-factly, "or to hurt her."

Billy shot up from his seat, his anger palpable. "I did no such thing."

"Sure you did," Stone said in a harsh tone. "You thought you'd scare her into...what? Stopping the old school from being torn down? Admitting she was to blame for the shooting?"

Billy dropped whatever he was rubbing between his fingers and bent to retrieve it. Riggs narrowed his eyes to try to see what it was, but the camera angle was off and he couldn't discern the object.

Stone pointed to the chair. "Sit down or I'll put you in handcuffs."

Billy dropped back into the chair with a curse and twisted his hands together. "You've got the wrong guy."

"Listen, Billy," Stone said, "I know what you said at her mother's funeral. I also have the note where you blamed her."

Billy's head jerked up. "What note?"

"This one." Stone laid the evidence bag on the table. The scribbled message *It was your fault* was clear through the bag.

Billy rocked back in his chair. "I didn't send that."

Riggs shifted, studying Billy's reaction. He seemed genuinely shocked.

"But you blamed Kate—"

"Yeah, I did. At least back then." Billy's frown deepened. "But that was over a decade ago. My life was hell." Pain contorted his face. "Everyone thought *I* helped my brother. Our classmates, people in town, even my own parents asked me if I'd known what he was up to and kept it quiet."

Pain underscored Billy's voice and he pinched the bridge of his nose.

"That must have been difficult," Stone said quietly.

"It sure as hell was," Billy said. "When my folks moved away, they treated me like I was a piranha. Maybe I did tease Ned when he was young, but he had problems no one knew about."

"What kind of problems?" Stone asked bluntly.

Billy pressed his lips together as if he was going to clam up.

"Tell me," Stone said. "It's time for the truth, Billy."

Billy laid his hands on the table, fingers curled into his palms. "When he was a baby, my daddy dropped him on his head. He didn't mean to, at least that's what I heard Mom say, but Ned must have hit his head hard. The doctor said he had a concussion. Later on, when he started acting all weird and depressed, they thought that head injury had caused his psychiatric problems."

Riggs pulled at his chin. Medical records were hard to obtain, but Stone could find a way to verify that information.

"What happened after you and your folks left Briar Ridge?" Stone asked.

Billy wiped at his eyes again. "They changed their names, tried to start a new life. But eventually folks would realize who they were or recognize them, and we'd move again. All that time, they just grew madder and madder. They couldn't stand to look at me. Then I started drinking." Billy shrugged. "Got a couple of DUIs, was living on the streets. Took odd jobs to get by."

He paused, and a long silence ensued. Finally, Stone muttered, "Go on."

"About a year and a half ago, I got a job at a trucking company, but my drinking almost cost me the work. Boss gave me an ultimatum. Lose the job or go to AA."

He opened his palm and reveled a sobriety chip. "Been sober now a year." He made a clicking sound with his teeth. "Part of the program is to make amends with those you hurt. That's the reason I wanted to talk to Kate. To tell her I'm sorry for blaming her." His voice warbled. "I know it wasn't her fault. Ned was troubled and bullied, but he had issues anyway. My sponsor helped me understand that."

"Do you know if Ned acted alone?" Stone asked.

Billy made a clicking sound with his teeth. "I honestly don't know."

"Did anything odd happen in the days before the shooting? Was Ned hanging out with anyone specific? Someone who might have given him the gun?"

"Not that he talked about, but Ned wasn't a talker."

"Other than Kate, was he upset with anyone else at school?"

Billy looked down at the chip then shook his head. "I never knew what was going on in his head. Two nights before the shooting, he came in acting all rattled. I asked him what was going on, but he wouldn't talk about it. But I had the weirdest vibe that he'd gotten laid." Billy sighed. "When I teased him about it, he went all crazy and ran out of the room. He didn't come back till the middle of the night. My folks were really pissed and grounded him."

"That was two days before the shooting?"

"Yeah, but I never learned what happened to set him off."

Riggs released a slow breath. He'd been certain Billy was trouble, but after hearing his story, he believed him.

Stone shoved a piece of paper in front of Billy. "One more thing. I need a writing sample. Copy the message."

Billy clenched the pen then copied the wording. It didn't take an analysis expert to determine that Billy's handwriting didn't match.

Stone suddenly stood and looked at his phone. "All right, Billy, you're free to go."

Riggs knotted his hands in frustration. If Billy was innocent, who the hell was trying to kill Kate?

KATE FROZE AT the sound of the man's voice. No, not exactly a man. A teenager. A student.

But she didn't understand why he was so upset or why he'd threaten her. "You don't really want to hurt me," she said, struggling to keep her voice calm. "What good will that do?"

"Just move," the teenager ordered.

He shoved her, and Kate stumbled toward the woods, mind racing. Amy would be back soon. And the mayor. Then other people would start arriving. But they might not be here in time.

She had to stall.

He gave her another push. "I said walk."

Kate moved toward the construction trailer, but with every step she was getting closer to her death. She'd faced it once during the shooting and survived.

She had to survive this time.

Riggs had been nothing but kind to her, and protective. He'd used his days off to make sure she was safe.

Yet she'd hurt him. She had to fix that.

She stumbled over a tree stump and fell, her hands digging into the brush. Inhaling a deep breath, she pivoted on the ground and looked up at the boy holding the gun.

"Why are you doing this?"

"You had to stir up the past with this new school celebration."

Kate narrowed her eyes. "I don't understand what that has to do with you. You weren't even around back then. You'll benefit by enjoying a new building."

Anger slashed his expression, his thin face stark with desperation. For a moment, she thought she saw something familiar in his face. Something that reminded her of another teenager she'd once known. Long ago.

One who had terrorized her and the other students at Briar Ridge High.

His menacing look. Eyes filled with desperation. The crazed look of someone out of his mind.

"Please, don't," she said. "Talk to me. Maybe I can help. Tell me why this project upsets you so much."

"Because you stirred up all the gossip and questions again," he said. "All the talk about him had died down. Finally."

Kate struggled to follow his logic. "Talk of Ned?"

He didn't have to answer. She saw it in his eyes. Pain. Shame. Rage.

"Why would talk about Ned Hodgkins bother you?"

"See, you're doing it, just like I thought," he screeched. "Asking about the past." He clenched his jaw and raised the gun.

Kate's breath caught in her throat as he pointed the barrel at her head.

Then he yanked her arm and dragged her toward the trailer. He pushed her inside, and she fell onto the sofa in the front office. His tennis shoes shuffled across the floor as he paced. "You shouldn't have invited everyone to come back to town," he snarled. "Now it's all everyone can talk about, and it's your fault."

Pausing in front of her, he removed a matchbook and struck a match. The mad look in his eyes intensified as he watched the flame burst to life.

For a moment, Kate sat frozen in horror as a panic attack threatened. She couldn't breathe, she was choking, her lungs straining for air.

She did not want to die.

Forcing a deep breath in to ward off the panic, she summoned her courage then lurched up and dove at the boy. With a wild grunt, he slammed the butt of the gun against her head, and she hit the floor on her hands and knees. Stars swam behind her eyes as she struggled to stand, but she was so dizzy she swayed and the world tilted. Then he yanked her by the arm and began to drag her toward the rear of the trailer...

RIGGS MET STONE in the hallway. Before he could speak, though, Stone's phone buzzed.

Stone connected the call. "Yeah. I'm on my way."

His deep frown made Riggs tense. "What's wrong?"

"Nine-one-one from the new building site. Mayor got there and saw smoke."

"What about Kate?"

"I don't know. Let's go." Stone ducked into the room where Macy was still studying the photographs. "Macy, there may be trouble at the new building site. It's Kate."

Macy's eyes widened and she reached for her shoulder bag. "I'm going with you."

The three of them hurried outside to Stone's police car and climbed in. Stone flipped on his siren and peeled from the parking lot.

Fear pulsed through Riggs. Dammit, if he hadn't been so stubborn and had stayed with Kate, she'd be safe.

If anything happened to her, he'd never forgive himself.

Stone's phone buzzed again and he pressed Connect. His deputy's voice echoed over the speakerphone. "Forensics called, Sheriff. The prints on the matchbook are not a match to Billy, Woody or to Don Gaines. Techs did find a partial on Kate's car that matched the one on the matchbook and on the bomb piping."

"So we're dealing with one perp?"

"Looks that way, although we don't have a name yet, which means he doesn't have priors."

Riggs silently cursed as Stone ended the call. "Then we're back to square one."

Sweat beaded on his neck as Stone sped down Main Street and veered onto Briar Ridge Circle. The moment they rounded the corner, Riggs spotted smoke billowing in the air.

"It's the construction trailer," Riggs muttered. "Kate had better not be in there."

Stone swerved up beside the mayor's Cadillac and threw the squad car into Park.

Stone removed his gun from his holster as he ran to the mayor, who was hovered near his car, on his phone. Macy pulled her gun and headed for the edge of the woods to search the area in case the perpetrator had escaped.

"Mayor," Stone said.

"I'll call you back." The mayor pocketed his phone, his face riddled with anxiety. "Fire department's on its way."

Riggs hit the ground running. Smoke seeped from what looked like a crack in the trailer window. He touched the metal door.

It was warm, but not hot. He didn't have much time. A small trailer like this could go up in minutes.

"I'll look for a back door or way in," Stone said as he disappeared around the side of the trailer.

Riggs turned the doorknob, but it was locked. "Kate!" Terrified for her, he shook the door and yanked on it. The metal rattled. Heat seeped through the door. "Kate, are you in there?"

Nothing but the sound of something inside rattling, then fire crackling. Damn, he had to hurry.

He raced over to the window and looked through the shattered glass. Cold fear and rage hit him. Flames danced through the room, but he couldn't see Kate.

She could be on the floor. Or in a damn closet.

"I'm coming, sweetheart," he murmured. He yanked

off his shirt, wrapped it around his hand and punched out the rest of the glass. Oxygen fed fire, so every second counted.

He dove through the window, smoke blurring his vision as he rolled across the floor. "I'm here, Kate! Where are you?" he shouted.

He jumped up and ran through the smoky fog, stomping at flames in his path. The fire was spreading, the blaze eating up the carpet and snapping at the curtains.

He raced through the room, darted across burning patches, and searched the closet. Empty.

Where was Kate?

Chapter Nineteen

A sizzling sound echoed from the bathroom of the trailer. Riggs's instincts surged to life. He jumped over a burning chair and yanked open the door. No Kate. Another pipe bomb. This one had nails attached.

Dammit to hell. It was about to go off.

Cursing, he ran back through the main room, shoved open the door and dove outside just as the trailer exploded. The fire engine careened into the parking lot, sirens wailing.

Stone jogged toward him. "Kate?"

"She's not inside," Riggs shouted.

"People are going to be here any minute." Stone scanned the parking lot. "If the perp has her, he probably took her somewhere."

There were no other cars around. Had he driven away with her?

Riggs pushed up from the ground, pulse pounding. "Where? We don't know who the hell we're dealing with."

"We'll find her," Stone said as the fire crew jumped from the truck and began to roll out the hoses.

A noise sounded from the woods to the right. Riggs pivoted to search the trees then stood bone-still and listened. Footsteps. Faint, but he heard them. Then a voice. A cry.

And movement.

If someone had forced Kate into the woods, he didn't want to alert them he was there. Although the siren had done that.

That meant the person who had Kate might be panicked. Desperate.

Panicked, desperate people did stupid things.

He glanced at Stone to get his attention, but he was talking to the mayor. Macy was out there somewhere in the woods. Maybe she'd find Kate.

Riggs crept toward the woods, slipping between the pines and oaks, eyes scanning.

The wind whistled. Brush rustled. A branch snapped off from a tall pine.

The voice again. Low. Shaky. Kate.

He inched pass a cypress, forcing himself to tread quietly, and continued walking until he spotted Kate. He went still, assessing the situation.

Kate threw up her hand as if pleading with her abductor to release her.

A thin, gangly guy in a dark gray hoodie had his back to Riggs, so he couldn't see the face. He had a gun, though, and was wildly waving it around.

"Think about your future," Kate said. "If you kill me, you'll go to prison."

"I—I won't have a future if it gets out who I am," the guy stammered.

"What do you mean who you are?" Kate said.

"Like I'd tell you or anyone else," he ranted. "Then I'd be crucified."

Riggs inched closer, hovering in the shadows.

"Think about your mother," Kate said, compassion in her tone. "How will she feel if you kill me?"

"She doesn't give a damn about me," the teen muttered.

"I doubt that's true," Kate said softly.

"It is," the boy shouted. "I was just some stupid mistake she made. I heard her say she wished she'd never had me. That she hated my father and was glad he was dead."

"Your father is dead?" Kate asked, confusion lacing her tone.

Riggs froze as the boy's face slipped into view. It was Roy Fulton.

Cassidy's son.

The amateur bomb, the fire behind Kate's house. All Roy.

Now he understood why Cassidy had kept Roy's father's identity quiet. She had been protecting her son. Not from his father, but from the stigma of his name and what Ned had done.

The boy paced in front of Kate, waving the gun like a madman. "Yeah, and you stirring up the past made everyone start talking about him again. That means people will start asking questions and they might find out."

"Find out what?" Kate asked.

Riggs slowly eased forward into the clearing. "That you're Ned's son, aren't you, Roy?"

KATE'S HEART POUNDED so hard she could hear the blood roaring in her ears. Roy Fulton was Ned's son? Riggs wasn't his father...

The boy swung around, gun aimed at Riggs, his eyes crazed. Déjà vu struck Kate. Roy had Ned's long, narrow chin, his high forehead. Why hadn't she seen it before?

"That's right!" Roy's hand shook. "And if everyone finds out, my life will be ruined. They'll think I'm just like him."

"You are just like him if you pull that trigger," Riggs said. "Ned killed innocent classmates and his teacher because he was angry. He had emotional problems and suffered a head injury when he was a baby. If you kill Kate or me, you can't use that as an excuse."

Roy's hand trembled as he glanced at Kate then back at Riggs. The gun bobbed up and down.

Compassion filled Kate's voice. "That must have been a shock. When did you find out Ned was your father?"

Roy dragged a hand over his face where tears trickled down his ruddy cheeks. "When Mama got the invitation to this stupid reunion. She was drunk and went on a rant about hating everyone in school. Then she just blurted it all out." Roy's voice cracked. "Said she and her girlfriend had a bet to see who could sleep with the most boys their senior year. Said Ned was the one she needed to win the bet. He was a nerd and awkward and gave in just like she knew he would. Then she laughed at him." Pain underscored Roy's words. "She laughs at me, too. Says I'm a weirdo like him."

"That's not true," Kate said. "You're smart, Roy, and talented on the computer. You can do something with that talent one day."

"Not if people find out I'm *his* son," Roy cried. "They'll hate me and run me out of town like they did Ned's family."

Riggs cleared his throat. "Did Ned know your mother was pregnant with his baby?"

Roy gave a sinister laugh. "She said when word spread she got knocked up, Ned asked her. She laughed and told him no way a weasel like him would be able to father a kid."

Dear God, Kate thought. Her cruel remarks must have crushed Ned.

"How can you be certain you're his son?" Riggs asked.

"She had one of those DNA tests done. I found it in the box she keeps under her bed."

"Oh, Roy, I'm so sorry," Kate said. "That must have hurt so much."

"You deserved better," Riggs said. "A mother who treated you with love and respect."

"Maybe she was protecting you by not telling you about Ned," Kate suggested softly. "She didn't want you to have to live in the shadow of what he'd done as his brother and his parents did."

Roy shot her a caustic stare. "It wasn't about me. She just didn't want anyone to know she'd slept with a loser like him," Roy muttered sarcastically. "Said she was afraid people would think she helped him plan the shooting."

"*Did* she?" Riggs asked.

Roy hesitated, maybe a little too long. "Hell, I don't know," Roy cried. "I mean, she hated some of the other kids, but she hates guns."

"Ned allowed things to destroy him and gave up. But you can rise above your problems and have a future," Kate said gently.

Roy shook his head back and forth. "No, I can't. I've already done too much. Your car and the fires..."

"No one was hurt though, so we'll work something out," Kate said softly. "You can get probation and receive counseling."

"She's right." Riggs held out his hand for the gun. "Don't let people in town remember you as a killer, Roy."

Roy's bony body trembled with emotions as he pushed his glasses up on his nose. Kate recognized the lost, empty, defeated look that suddenly shadowed his eyes.

The same look Ned had had before he'd opened fire.

But instead of shooting her or Riggs, Roy turned the gun on himself.

Macy and Stone both stepped into the clearing, guns raised, eyes on Roy. "Drop the gun," Macy said calmly.

"Roy, no!" Kate cried. "Please don't—"

She didn't get to finish the sentence. Riggs tackled Roy, sending the boy to the ground as they struggled for the weapon.

Then a gunshot.

Kate froze in horror as blood spilled onto the ground.

RIGGS GRUNTED AND pushed the kid off him. Blood soaked his shirt as well as Roy's.

The teen had been hit in the shoulder and was howling like an injured animal.

Footsteps crunched leaves and dirt as Macy ran toward them and kicked the gun to the side. Stone sprinted up a second later.

Riggs rolled to his knees, ripped the bottom of his T-shirt and pressed it to Roy's shoulder.

"You're going to be okay, kid," Riggs said.

Kate rushed over, her face horrified. "Riggs?"

"He's all right. The bullet pierced his shoulder, not a main artery or his heart."

Kate knelt beside him. "How about you? Are you hurt?"

"I'm good."

Macy approached them, putting her gun back in its holster. "Kate, are you hurt?"

Kate's gaze met Macy's, and the years fell away as she murmured she was okay. They were five years old again, huddled in the dark in her room while a storm brewed. She wanted to go to her and pull her into a hug, but Macy still seemed to be holding back.

"An ambulance is on the way," Stone said.

"It hurts," Roy wailed.

"Just be grateful you're alive and didn't kill anyone," Riggs said, his sympathy for the kid warring with the fear that had nearly immobilized him at the sight of that gun pointed at Kate.

Kate stroked Roy's hair from his forehead. "Medical help is on the way, Roy."

"But I'll go to jail," he whined.

"You might," Stone cut in. "But you'll also get the help you need."

"I'll call your mother," Riggs promised. Maybe this would bring the two of them closer together.

A siren wailed and Stone hurried off to lead the paramedics to their location while he phoned Cassidy and told her to meet her son at the hospital.

Riggs, contemplating what Roy had done, also understood his reasons. The kid needed a father figure, or at least a big brother.

Maybe he'd offer to help get him in a treatment program. He could even mentor the boy, help teach him about being a man.

And Stone would follow up to see if Cassidy had known what Roy had intended.

Brush rattled and voices echoed, indicating the medics were approaching. Other cars sounded as they arrived, and Macy went to ensure there was no more trouble.

After they loaded Roy on the stretcher, one of them checked Kate where Roy had hit her with the gun. Thankfully, she was bruised but didn't need stitches.

Riggs stood, ready to follow Roy to the ambulance, but Kate caught his arm. His shirt was bloody and sweat soaked his skin.

"Thank God, you're all right, Riggs." She searched his face. "I'm so sorry for what I said earlier, for believing those rumors. I know you're not that man. The last few days, I've realized how strong and brave you are."

Footsteps sounded again, the mayor jogging toward them. "People are starting to arrive, Kate!"

Riggs squeezed her hand. "Let's go. You've worked hard for this." And nearly sacrificed her life.

She squeezed his hand. "We'll talk later, Riggs. Please."

He nodded, his throat thickening. Images of the shooting that had changed the town had struck him the moment he'd seen Roy with the gun.

Today, Roy could have taken Kate from him.

He had survived the trauma of nearly losing his leg when Ned had shot him.

He didn't think he'd survive if he'd lost Kate.

KATE WAS STILL trembling from the ordeal with Roy as she walked up to the outdoor stage.

Cars rumbled into the lot and parked, residents and alumni climbing from their vehicles and gathering on the lawn. Amy, shaken when she realized what had happened, had returned and quickly set up the refreshment table.

Kate spotted Brynn near the front of the crowd, her mother hovering by her side. Friends and groups from school had reconnected and hung together. Macy stood by Stone, their heads bent in conversation. But Trey wasn't with her.

Maybe that was a good sign.

Before the mayor started the dedication, Kate scanned the crowd for Riggs. He'd changed shirts and looked so handsome her breath stalled in her chest. His gaze locked with hers, and he gave her a small nod of encouragement.

His approval and support bolstered her confidence, and she joined the mayor at the podium.

"We're delighted to have such a nice turnout today. The town council, along with Kate McKendrick and the committee she spearheaded, have worked tirelessly to bring this event to fruition. First, Kate will say a few words about the memorial, then we'll start the festivities."

He stepped aside and Kate moved in behind the microphone. She welcomed everyone and thanked them for coming. "I'm excited today about the future of Briar Ridge and our young people. As I said before, I believe this new school will energize our students and families and inspire optimism as well as draw new families to the area." Kate swallowed, an image of her mother's face haunting her. Sunshine broke through the clouds. For a brief second, she could have sworn she saw her mother smiling at her, a proud gleam in her eyes.

"To honor those students we lost, we created a memorial for the front wall of the school. It will be the first thing students and visitors see when they enter the new Briar Ridge High. The shadow boxes are filled with photographs and quotes from loved ones and friends honoring the students."

She paused. "Beside the wall of shadow boxes there will be a special section featuring photos of other students and alumni, showcasing their accomplishments. Each of you, each of us, deserves a badge of courage for proving the shooting didn't destroy us. It's my hope that this wall will inspire students to overcome their own tragedies and obstacles to pursue their dreams." Each of the victims who'd lost their life was featured in one section while another held photographs and the stories of survivors. Stone's brother Mickey was there, along with Riggs and Brynn. Even Orson.

She gestured toward the display. "On the other display board, we've included blueprints for the new sports fields and stadium. Please take the time to look at the plans and the memorial." She motioned to the mayor. "Now, Mayor Gaines will officially cut the ribbon then Sheriff Lawson will break ground."

Voices rumbled, followed by applause. Kate's breath quickened, her fears dissipating at the smiles of approval. She and Amy joined the mayor where a red, blue and white ribbon had been stretched between two white posts.

"Here's to new beginnings in Briar Ridge and at Briar Ridge High School." Mayor Gaines lifted the scissors and cut the ribbon, bringing cheers.

As the applause died down, Kate gestured at the time capsule. "Fifteen years ago, the members of the senior class were asked to write a letter to themselves that described their goals and dreams and where they envisioned they'd be. We're going to open the time capsule now."

Voices echoed through the crowd as Kate asked Stone to do the honors. He and a team had built the metal capsule in one of the metal- and wood-crafting classes their senior year.

Stone pried the lid off the capsule. "Miss Turner is

going to hand out the letters while we mingle and have refreshments. I hope everyone enjoys seeing what their younger selves wrote."

Kate accepted hers and stepped aside to read it while Amy passed out the others. Voices and laughter spread, some expressing disappointment over unattained dreams, others laughing about their teenaged wistful thoughts.

Kate studied the words she'd scrawled on the page.

Dear Kate,
By the time you read this, I hope you've accomplished your dreams. You'll be a teacher and help shape lives just as Mom does. Macy and Brynn and you will still be best friends, and you'll share coffee and conversations while your children run and play on the playground and have sleepovers.

Yes, Kate, you won't be a shy, awkward girl anymore. You'll stop lingering in the shadows and stand up for what you believe in. You'll also go after what you want.

Most of all, I hope you're happy, Kate, that you've found the love of your life. I see you with a big house full of children you'll shower with love. And a man who will appreciate your uniqueness.

Kate blinked tears away as she finished reading the message her younger self had written. She had accomplished part of her dreams. She had taught school and was the principal now. She helped shape young lives.

But she, Brynn and Macy weren't close anymore.

She squared her shoulders and vowed to rectify that.

Riggs was standing by the time capsule, reading his own message.

Young Kate had dreamed about marriage and a family and love.

She wanted that now, too.

She just had to have the courage to go after what she wanted.

Chapter Twenty

Riggs had forgotten what he'd written to himself. But he chuckled as he skimmed the note.

He'd had lofty dreams of being a professional athlete, had imagined making the US Olympic team. He'd wanted fame, and women, and planned to travel the world instead of settling down.

He hissed a breath. Back then, he'd been arrogant and innocent, and full of boyish dreams.

He wasn't that boy any longer. He was a man.

His heart tripped in his chest as he looked at Kate. He wanted different things now.

He wanted Kate and all the strings attached.

But there were too many people here to have a private chat. She was walking toward him, though, so he met her halfway. His breath caught as she clasped his hand.

"Are you okay?" he asked.

She nodded. "I feel badly for Roy."

"Everybody makes their choices." Riggs cleared his throat. "Kate, about homecoming?"

She shrugged. "I didn't go in high school."

He pressed her hand to his chest. "Will you be my date tonight?

A soft smile lit her eyes then she murmured *yes*. He was tempted to kiss her, but a commotion erupted by a row of cars in the parking lot.

Stone hurried to the scene, and Riggs and Kate arrived just in time to watch Macy slap handcuffs on Trey Cushing.

KATE'S HEART STUTTERED as Stone rushed to Macy's side. "What's going on?"

Macy jerked Trey's arm and forced him to face the crowd. "I found evidence. Trey gave Ned the .38 Special he used in the shooting."

"I didn't know what he'd planned to do," Trey bellowed.

"You're still under arrest as an accomplice to murder," Macy snapped.

Shocked whispers rattled through the alumni as Macy shoved Trey inside the back of Stone's squad car. Stone and Macy then climbed into the front seat and sped away.

Kate sighed in relief. They finally had the answer they'd needed about Ned's accomplice.

Billy approached, his expression contrite. "Kate?"

She tensed, but Riggs gave her arm a squeeze. "Listen to him, Kate. I think you need to hear what he has to say."

Kate took a deep breath, then nodded at Billy. "Okay."

Billy shifted nervously, but finally made eye contact.

"Kate, I wanted to apologize to you for what I said, for blaming you for what my brother did."

Kate softened at his sincere tone.

"I was young and stupid, and my parents blamed me so I passed the buck." He lifted a chip that she recognized as an AA chip. "I'm sorry. Really sorry."

The guilt Kate had lived with eased. "Thank you for saying that, Billy."

"I'm trying to do better. Both for me and for Ned."

A smile warmed her heart. "Good for you."

Amy waved at her and motioned to the podium where Kate was surprised to see Jimmy standing. He looked worn and frail, but he pounded his knuckles on the podium and everyone turned to see what was going on.

"By now," Jimmy said as the crowd hushed, "you all should have received the letters I sent."

Kate gaped at him. Letters?

"I attended the very school you're tearing down, and I've worked there for over two decades. During that time, I've seen good kids and some not so nice ones." His voice shook. "I watched what you all did to Ned, how your ignored and teased him. My classmates did the same thing to me, and I never got over it."

The mayor inched closer to Jimmy, but Jimmy raised a hand. "I ain't here to hurt anybody. But since Kate called this reunion, I thought everyone should be reminded of who was to blame." He pointed his finger across the crowd, one by one. "You and you and you and you…" He pressed his hand to his chest. "And now we've seen another boy arrested today, another boy lost. When is it going to end?"

Tears filled Kate's eyes and she joined Jimmy on the stage. "We're working on it, Jimmy. I promise, we're working on it."

KATE WAS JUST finishing dressing for the homecoming dance when her doorbell buzzed. She checked her reflection and smiled at herself in the mirror, although she wished she'd had time to buy a new dress.

Who would have ever guessed that she would finally go to homecoming with handsome Riggs Benford?

The bell buzzed again and she hurried to answer it. Instead of Riggs, Macy and Brynn were at her door. Hope budded in Kate's heart.

Without a wheelchair ramp, Macy had helped Brynn up the porch steps.

Macy's face crumpled and Brynn sniffed. "Can we come in and talk?" Macy asked.

Kate nodded, emotions welling in her throat, and together she and Macy assisted Brynn inside and settled her into a chair. Kate had longed to see her friends for so long that words failed her.

"Brynn called me after we arrested Trey..." Macy began.

Kate narrowed her eyes and looked back and forth between them.

"Kate," Brynn said, "I'm so sorry."

Kate swallowed hard. "What's going on?"

"You weren't the only one who received a letter of blame," Macy said. "Brynn and I both did, and so did some other alumni. That's one reason I came back. To find out who sent it."

Kate rubbed her fingers together. "Jimmy did it. He wanted us all to think about how we treated each other."

"I know." Brynn knotted her hands in her lap. "I deserved it, Kate. It was partly my fault Ned went on that shooting spree."

"No, Brynn, Ned was troubled. He had a head injury from childhood that caused him to have emotional issues."

Brynn's eyes widened. She hadn't known.

"But I spread gossip about him to Gretta." Brynn's voice cracked. "It...it was stupid, but I never thought Ned would go crazy and get a gun." Tears ran down Brynn's cheeks. "Your mother...you lost her because of me..."

"No, she died because of me," Macy said in a pained whisper. "Ned turned the gun on me, but your mother stepped in front of me and took the bullet instead." A sob escaped Macy. "I'm so sorry, Kate. That's why I left town. Your mother was so good to me, she loved me more than my own mother did. I couldn't bear to face you. I figured you'd hate me."

"Oh, God," Kate murmured. "Neither one of you is at fault." She looked at Brynn. "I thought you blamed me for putting you in that wheelchair."

"No," Brynn cried. "I just felt so bad about your mother, and then..."

"And you couldn't walk," Kate said. "I wish it had been me, Brynn, instead of you."

"Oh, Kate, I never thought or wanted that," Brynn said.

Her mother's face stared down at her from the mantel. "You know, Mom wouldn't want us blaming our-selves," Kate said. "She'd want us to be together."

Macy and Brynn both nodded and the three of them fell together in a group hug just like they had when they were little girls.

Nothing would ever tear them apart again.

Anthony Clancy went with. If Brynn were going to stay then she would need to find help for Kate, and Brynn said she would make to reach her. Whether his friendship would make it all the way through to the end, but at least Kate was pulling might even get him to part again.

Chapter Twenty-One

It took Kate an hour to repair her makeup after Macy and Brynn left, but it was worth it. Brynn had even brought her an outfit to wear for the homecoming, a V-necked green satin cocktail dress that hugged her curves in all the right places and sparkly silver heels.

She'd also told them she was moving into a small apartment on her own, that it was time to get out from under her mother's smothering. Kate and Macy promised to be there for her. It was something Kate was looking forward to.

Kate entered the homecoming party on Riggs's arm, elated that she and her friends had reconciled.

The clubhouse was filled with alumni, the mood tonight shifting as if the weight of the past had finally been lifted. Maybe forgiveness would bring them all even closer.

"Cassidy insists she didn't know what Ned planned," Stone told her.

"So she lied and triggered his breakdown, but she can't be charged for that," Kate said. "Not any more than the rest of us."

"No, it's time to move on." Riggs pulled her onto the dance floor and they swayed to the soft lull of music. She spotted Stone dancing with Macy, and Jay Eastwood had scooped Brynn up from her wheelchair and was dancing her across the floor with a look of adoration. Maybe they were all three going to find romance now. And complete their dream of being in each other's weddings.

"I've been waiting a long time to do this," Riggs murmured as he swung her around.

Kate threaded her fingers in his hair. "I'm sorry for believing that rumor about you and Cassidy."

Riggs shook his head, regret darkening his eyes. "I should have told you," he murmured, "but my pride got in the way. I wanted you to see me for who I am now, to realize that I never would have abandoned a baby, not even back then."

"I do see that, Riggs," Kate murmured. "I guess I let my own past get in the way."

He gently tucked a strand of her hair behind her ear. "What do you mean?"

"My father left my mom when he found out she was pregnant. I…never knew him. And he never wanted any part of me."

"Oh, God, Kate," Riggs said gruffly. "I'm sorry. I didn't know."

Kate shrugged. "You'd think it wouldn't have affected me, but it did. And then losing Mom. I was afraid to love and lose again."

"I know what you mean," he murmured. "Sometimes our pasts have a way of interfering with our futures," Riggs said. "And not in a good way."

She lifted a hand and pressed it against his cheek. "But other times, in the best ways. The past shaped you into a hero."

"I'm no hero," he said in a self-deprecating tone.

Kate smiled. "You are to me." Her voice cracked. "I don't want to lose you, Riggs."

"Ah, Kate, you've got me as long as you want me," Riggs said in a sexy whisper. "I want to go to bed with you and wake up with you every morning." He brushed his thumb across her cheek. "I want to marry you and have children with you and grow old together."

Tears blurred Kate's eyes and she looped her arms around his neck. "And sit in those rockers on your front porch and watch our children play."

He chuckled. "And cuddle with them under the quilts my mother made."

Emotions crowded Kate's throat. "I would love that."

Then he dragged her into his arms and kissed her.

* * * * *

Look for more books in
USA TODAY *bestselling author Rita Herron's*
Badge of Courage miniseries coming soon!

SPECIAL EXCERPT FROM

♦ HARLEQUIN

INTRIGUE

*When a murder investigation reunites
Deputy Della Howard with her ex,
Sheriff Barrett Logan, she knows remaining
professional is crucial to solving this case. But as a
trained investigator, how long will it be before
Logan figures out she's carrying his child...*

Keep reading for a sneak peek at
Her Child to Protect,
the first book in a brand-new series,
Mercy Ridge Lawmen, from
USA TODAY *bestselling author Delores Fossen.*

"Oh, God," she said, the words fighting with her gusting breath. "I
need you to take me to the hospital now. I've been shot."

Della forced herself to slow her breathing. Panicking wouldn't
help and would only make things worse. Still, it was hard to hold
it together when she felt the pain stabbing through her and saw the
blood.

The baby.

The fear of losing her child roared through her like an
unstoppable train barreling at her. The injury wasn't that serious.
Definitely not life-threatening. But any loss of blood could also
mean a miscarriage.

Della nearly blurted out for Barrett to hurry, that it wasn't just
her arm injury at stake, but there was no need. Barrett was already
hurrying, driving as fast as he safely could, and he was doing that
while on the phone with Daniel to get his brother and a team out
looking for that SUV. And for the men who'd just tried to kill them.

For as long as she could remember, she'd wanted to be a cop. And wearing the badge meant facing danger just like this. But everything was different now that her baby was added to the mix. She couldn't lose his child. It didn't matter that the pregnancy hadn't been planned or that Barrett didn't want to be a father. She had to be okay so that her baby would be, too.

She managed to text Jace, to tell him that she and Barrett were heading back to the hospital and that he should do the same. Especially since Daniel would have the pursuit of the gunmen under control. Besides, she wanted Jace at the hospital in case those thugs came after Alice.

"How bad are you hurting?" Barrett asked when he ended the call with Daniel.

Della shook her head, hesitating so that she could try to get control of her voice. "It's okay."

It wasn't, of course. There was pain, but if she tried to describe it to Barrett, she might spill all about the baby. This wasn't the way she wanted him to find out. Later, after she'd been examined. Maybe after the shooters had been caught, she'd tell him then.

Thankfully, they weren't that far from the hospital, only a few minutes, and when Barrett pulled into the parking lot, he drove straight to the doors of the ER. Someone had alerted them, probably Daniel, because the moment Barrett came to a stop, a nurse and an EMT came rushing out toward them. Even though Della could have walked on her own, they put her on a gurney and rushed her into the hospital.

Barrett was right behind them.

Don't miss
Her Child to Protect *by Delores Fossen,*
available May 2021 wherever
Harlequin Intrigue books and ebooks are sold.

Harlequin.com

HIEXP0421